BAKUNIN'S SON

BAKUNIN'S SON

by

Sergio Atzeni

Translated by John H. Rugman

ITALICA PRESS
NEW YORK
1996

ITALIAN ORIGINAL
IL FIGLIO DI BAKUNIN
1991 © SELLERIO EDITORE VIA SIRACUSA 50 PALERMO

TRANSLATION COPYRIGHT © 1996 BY JOHN H. RUGMAN

ITALICA PRESS, INC.
595 MAIN STREET
NEW YORK, NEW YORK 10044

All rights reserved. No part of this publication may be reproduced, stored in a retrieval system, or transmitted, in any form or by any means, electronic, mechanical, photocopying, recording, or otherwise, without the prior permission of Italica Press.

Library of Congress Cataloging-in-Publication Data

Atzeni, Sergio.
 [Figlio di Bakunin. English]
 Bakunin's son / by Sergio Atzeni ; translated by John H. Rugman.
   p. cm.
 ISBN 0-934977-44-5 (pbk. : alk. paper)
 I. Rugman, John H., 1963– . II. Title.
 PQ4861.T94F513 1996
 853'.914--dc20   96-16576
                                                                CIP

Printed in the United States of America
5 4 3 2 1

Cover Illustration: "Photographs of Persons Subject to Special Surveillance at the Borders." Paris, Musée de la Police.

Please note…facts, characters, Madonnas dressed in black, and locations (even when the names of villages, quarters, and streets correspond to actual places) in the following pages are entirely fictional. Any attempt at recognizing real people or events will prove futile. I do however beg your pardon for the small bit of truth you find herein, it was not written out of malice.

I

Last night I dreamed of Tullio Saba. The skin on his face was like wax, his eyes were wide open, scared, maybe a little sad.... He had an American military shirt on, from the war, torn to shreds. He said to me, "Everyone's forgotten me, my friends, even my women."

Haven't I ever spoken to you of him? He was a good guy. Miner. Comrade, head of the local party. A little crazy.

He courted me, right after the war.

I liked your father better.

Strange that I dreamed about him. I wonder what it means. Dreaming of the dead doesn't necessarily bring bad luck...maybe it was a kind of forewarning? Something that comes from far away, or returns from the past?

Do you want me to tell you his story? How we met?

You're curious about him...your father was never this curious, never asked me anything...you're more jealous of Tullio Saba than he ever was.

Most of Tullio Saba's vicissitudes are a mystery to me. And even if I knew...oh, but I can't tell a story right, I start rambling and everything gets all tangled up.... If I had to pick a place to begin, well, maybe I'd tell you about those little hats that Annarita and I cut and sewed ourselves to wear on our evening stroll under the porticoes, in '46, and how we only put them on once and never again....

Go to Guspini, the people of Guspini have a good memory. Yes, his fellow townsfolk know everything. If you ask them, they'll tell you. You'll find out what's left of a man after his death, in the memories and words of others.

Sergio Atzeni

Maybe that way he'll stop coming in my dreams and giving me such a hard time.

2

Saba, the one who sold wine?
No?
His brother, the one who married Arremundu Corriazzu's sister?
No?
His father?
No?
His father's brother, the one who killed three rabid dogs in the country and found a gold chain?
No?
The father's brother's son died in the war, I didn't know him.
The only Saba I knew personally was the one who sold wine.

3

I don't remember any Saba. Forty years in the mines, at San Giovanni, no Saba. The Sabas that I knew sold wine and made shoes, but in the mines nobody.... Wait a minute! Edigardu Saba! Yeah, him. Seems to me he put in three years there, at San Giovanni, but that wasn't the life for him. He was lazy, a sly devil. Three years, then they fired him, he went to sell razors and combs in Arbus. I always said, Folks in Arbus are stupid. Then he died young and left behind a milk store, in Arbus. His son lost it playing poker with Wilson. Wilson sold it to another guy from Arbus and made thousands on the deal.

You don't know Wilson? Peppi Mustazzolu's son. Wilson, he's famous. You know anyone in Cagliari? Wilson, a great gambler, one of those guys who knows every card and pool trick in the book. Now he lives in Aristanis, but there was a time when he had gambling houses in Asmara, when we had the colonies. Smart man. He lived thanks to the imbeciles. When he couldn't find anyone to fleece, he didn't lose hope.

Once he finds himself flat broke, what does he do? He rents himself a dark gentleman's suit, rents a brand new Mercedes, goes to Salvatore Poddighe, the one from Baratili, who's got Vernaccia like no one else can make, wine fit for a king, and gets himself two fifty-liter casks of aged Vernaccia, the real good stuff — all on credit, the suit, the car, the gas, the wine, cause at that time Wilson didn't have a penny to his name. He sets off. He goes to Gallura, where the Aga Kahn had just arrived — they'd put his picture in the paper. Wilson gets there and introduces himself to the Aga Kahn, speaking English like he was born in America. He seemed like a millionaire, the way he presented himself, saying he wanted to give the foreign guest a little taste of Vernaccia. "Taste it, taste it," he says to him, but the Aga Kahn doesn't drink wine — turns out he never ate or drank anything not tasted first by his servants, for fear of being poisoned. So the servants tasted, and tasted, and finished off the hundred liters. Wilson became the supplier of Vernaccia di Baratili to all the big wheels up that way and got himself back on track. Wasn't long before he was selling Sard wine to half the world. Really now, at Cagliari y'all don't know him? It's true, though, at Cagliari only the jerks get famous.

Sergio Atzeni

4

I never knew him personally, only by reputation. He was a communist.

I knew his father personally, a good man, an excellent shoemaker. The father's brother I knew better, Peppi Saba, best carriage maker in all Campidano. At that time there still weren't any cars in Campidano, and Peppi was rich. By the time cars arrived Peppi was old and little by little had squandered all the money he'd accumulated up till then. When it was gone, he died. He was younger than me. How can I be so old and still be on the ball? Eating, drinking, and minding my own beeswax, that's how.

Peppi was honest. I never heard that he stole anything. Never. Even during the war, when a lot of people....

This is what I can say about the Saba family, and what everybody else says too: the Sabas were crazy. No one ever said they were dishonest or bad craftsmen. A bunch of nuts who never hurt anyone. The men tended to be quite dissipated. They weren't stingy. The women were cheerful — wild, but cheerful. That's the Sabas for you. And that's why I was against it when my grandson wanted to marry a Saba. He didn't follow my advice, and today the village can't even keep track of how many times his wife's cheated on him. If my wife ever wanted to go out of the house, I'd give her a good kick and send her to bed. You know how women are. Don't let up on the reins or they'll pull 'em right out of your hands. Today...the women are taking over the world...we're doomed.

Bakunin's Son

5

Tullio Saba was a very egotistical child. Many times I caught him posing in front of the only mirror in the house, on the dresser in Donna Margherita's bedroom. It was an exaggeratedly ornate mirror, with a gilded stucco frame, and on top a fat little naked angel. For a well-mannered woman, Donna Marghertia posed in front of that mirror a little too much herself. The boy always had fine shoes, black and shiney — okay, his father was a shoemaker, but still, no kid in town had shoes as nice. And though the father was no tailor, no kid dressed as elegantly either. I recall a certain black corduroy suit — it had a red hem embroidered with flowers and fruit, made him look like a cross between a baby girl and a baron's son. And the short pants! Like the rich kids from the continent! I went to Cagliari three or four times before the war, and even there I never saw a kid so well-dressed, not even the nobles' children were done up as fancy as little Tullio Saba.

He was such a beautiful child, the most beautiful child in the village, with eyes black and sly, that darted round like a fox's. Ever since he was a kid he thought he was God's gift to the world; the spitting image of his father, a couple of dreamers. Those Sabas, their heads got big alright, during the good years. But if you blow yourself up too much you're bound to pop. When somebody's already rich and aristocratic, that's one thing — the people of the village won't criticize you, your servants won't whisper. But if you're born like Antoni Saba, grandson of a serf, who one day has a little good luck shine on him and gets a big head about it, well, what good can possibly come from it? Tragedy! Grandson of a serf, that's right; yes, his grandfather

Sergio Atzeni

was a field hand and back in those days that was the same as being a serf. The Sabas used to talk of ancient times, when their ancestors were gentlemen and masters, great landowners with herds of livestock and serfs, all robbed one day by foreign invaders. I wasn't around in ancient times. However, I don't really believe the Sabas were aristocratic gentlemen at all. Just a bunch of stories. I imagined that the evil they succumbed to would be like an ambush, punishing them for their vanity. I expected it. I prayed for them, especially for the boy. Nobody can grow up right in that kind of arrogant atmosphere.... And the money they wasted on me, a mere servant and cook, wages that not even a schoolteacher could earn back then. Teaching the ABCs is more important than cooking up panadas. The Sabas sure liked my panadas though, and I knew how to make 'em the way they're supposed to be made — I was born in Assemini, and the first smell that greeted me as I came into this world was panadas, with a crispy crust on the outside, soft on the inside, like my mamma used to make 'em — I learned from her, what days those were, boy! If there's a place known for its panadas, that's Assemini.

When I was in service at the Sabas, the richest man in the village was Totoi Zuddas. He had land, houses, olives, fruit trees, sheep, cows, dogs, donkeys. Really rich. Everyone pays for his good luck in some way or another, and Signor Zuddas was the father of seven daughters. He never spent one red cent on dressing his girls better than the other girls — just the opposite! He put those girls to work, sent them out to the vinyard with his fieldhands to harvest grapes. Tullio Saba, on the other hand, was dressed like a prince and taught to read and write.

Bakunin's Son

Every Saturday we had Signor Gaston over for dinner. He was a Frenchman, director of the mine. Now there was a real gentleman for you. I had to work double on those nights, heard my name called a hundred times — Dolores, the sauce! Dolores, the agnolotti! Dolores, mix the riccotta with the beets! Dolores, the panadas! Dolores, did you carve the goat yet? For the stuffing for the panadas every Saturday they killed two baby goats. I don't want to malign the Sabas or anything, but two baby goats every Saturday! Dolores Murtas never maligned anybody — I'm no witch — but I saw what went on in that house and said to myself, their luck's gonna finish in ashes someday. The way they spoke at the dinner table — running in and out from the kitchen the whole time I couldn't help but overhear the things they said, even though I didn't want to listen. Let me tell you, it's no good to talk that way. Antoni Saba spoke badly of the king. And of the pope! And the government. In those days there lived a famous arsonist whose name was Bakunin. During every conversation Antoni Saba mentioned this Bakunin, sprinkling his name here and there like using parsley in the kitchen.

Christmas Eve is a holy night, when all good men are supposed to be on their best behavior — that's the night our Lord was born. It shouldn't be a servant to have to teach these things. But one Christman Eve Antoni Saba left the house drunk, went down to the piazza where everyone could hear him, and started yelling at the top of his voice: "If Bakunin comes to Guspini," just like that he says, I remember it word for word, "drinks are on me, and I'll give him a place to sleep same as if he was my brother! And if Bakunin says to me, 'Antoni, why don't we burn down the church?' I'll answer, 'Let's go, Bakunin,' and I'll light the kindling for him!" Drunkards talk nothing but foolishness, okay, but Antoni Saba was serious. He would have taken fine

Sergio Atzeni

care of Bakunin, would have wined and dined him, and he really would have lit the kindling for him. That's why Don Sarais, the parish priest back then, got up on the pulpit Christmas day and explained to everybody that Bakunin was a real live arsonist, a dangerous criminal wanted by the police, who hid in Switzerland because the Swiss hide all the delinquents, traveled the world like an aristocrat, he was Russian, and all those cursed arsonists were Russian, and if he happened to show his face in Guspini he'd burn the church down and declare anarchy. Don Sarais even explained what anarchy was: the killing of the priests, raping of well-mannered women, pillaging of the farm houses, declaration of free love — a society geared toward the creation of a world of bimbo dames with no modesty and men without the fear of God. From that Christmas on, the whole village nicknamed Antoni Saba "Bakunin."

Everyone called him "Bakunin" and he was happy about it. "I'm going to Bakunin's to get me a pair of shoes made," they used to say. At making shoes he was the tops, and he deserves recognition for this. No shoemaker like him, not in Cagliari, not in Buggerru. That's the reason Signor Gaston bought shoes for the miners from him. His were the only shoes that didn't soak through down in the shafts. Signor Gaston sold them in the commissary, deducted the cost of the shoes from the miners wages.

Sturdy shoes, well-made. During this period of great dinners at the house, Antoni Saba employed twenty-one workers and was very rich. Even though I was a mere servant, I thought: it's one thing to be rich off the land, the land won't betray you; but quite another thing is the wealth accumulated by a lucky shoemaker. Good luck lived in that house. But I could hear the bad luck coming, it used to whistle in the drafts that blew through the doors. The Sabas were too different from the others, too vain. Donna Margherita insisted on being called "Donna" as if she were an aristocrat, and she was no aristocrat — she was the daughter of Ogliastrine shepards, maybe even bandits. Every Tuesday she hired a carriage and went down to Buggerru to buy shirts and veils, French skirts, immodest — and this started before she married Saba. When Buggerru became a ghost town, and later, when her daughters were born, and then when Tullio, who was the most spoiled of them all, came along, she ordered her clothes through the mail from a fashion house that had had a store in Buggerru during the golden years, when even in Buggerru there were clothes stores and painted women just like in Paris. Of all the women in Guspini only Donna Margherita out-dressed the director of the mine's wife, Signora Gaston (Signor Gaston was French and had a French wife). That's how the Sabas were, no shame, no measure.

 One day, I remember it like it was today, Totoi Zuddas' men came back from the fields and told how a worker from Ussana (there've always been bad folks from Ussana) tried to have his way with Isadora, the eldest Zuddas daughter. But she whipped out a pair of grape harvesting scissors and cut off his precious parts! That's how Totoi Zuddas' girls were, well-mannered. On the other hand, to show you the difference, that same evening, or maybe the next day, I saw Fiametta Saba, Antoni's eldest girl, clinging to a field hand as they sat very cozily under an almond tree outside of town — and she had her shirt lifted up! I didn't go out to spy on them, God be my witness, Dolores Murtas is no spy; I'd gone out to gather some mirto for the taccula — you can't eat taccula without mirto and salt. It was that same year, cause by then sins abounded so that the heavens nearly turned away in shame, Signor Gaston (and his wife) returned to France.

Sergio Atzeni

A new director of the mine came, a black-shirt Fascist. In no time at all he cut out buying shoes from Antoni Saba. He had shoes brought in from the continent. So "Bakunin" fired his workers one by one. When he finished with them, I left on my own free will, to serve another master, in Arbus. It wasn't two years before someone brought news that Antoni Saba had killed himself. I wasn't surprised.

6

I was a kid when I first met Tullio Saba, then for many years I didn't see him. I don't have a precise recollection of him. I heard my father talk about his father, they were friends even if they didn't have the same ideas. My father said, "I like the way Antoni Saba talks," and I think maybe he also liked the good cooking in that house, and quite a few good wines that could be found only at the Saba's. There was a Nasco di Quartu, which he always spoke of, compared it to our wines, and said, "Now that is wine for a gentleman, it doesn't cloud your brain." I remember that because he said it many times. Daddy was afraid of the bad opinions of the other villagers, he didn't care to be the object of chatter and gossip, and every time he talked about his friendship with old Antoni he would add, "My son, if anyone asks you, tell 'em that Bachisio Meloni is no anarchist. He's a friend of Bakunin Saba because they've lived on the same street for thirty years, and Bakunin Saba's never done him any harm."

Once, the priest back then, Don Sarais, was to confirm my sister Pina and called my daddy into the rectory to tell him that if he continued his friendship with the Antichrist he wouldn't

Bakunin's Son

confirm my sister and when the time came wouldn't marry any of us kids. My father promised to cut off the friendship — what else could he have done? He respected the Sacraments. After, he still went to his friend's, just made sure it was pitch dark when he went, that's all, so no one would be able to see him and rat on him to the priest. Daddy didn't like to lie, it's just that Don Sarais wouldn't have understood.... To give you an idea about the priest, some folks in the village said that his eyebrow was at an angle on account of he was always spying all over the place, and he had elephant ears because he was always listening behind closed doors, eavesdropping. Anyhow, they respected him because he was the priest — if you wanted the Sacraments you had to go to him. But as a man, he was strongly criticized....

Old Antoni's funeral I remember well. Tullio was still a boy, maybe fourteen years old; he walked stiff like he had a broomstick stuck up his butt, right behind the coffin, eyes dry, holding up his mother who cried. Behind them were a few relatives and maybe twenty or so miners. The reasons for the Saba's bad luck were no mystery; these were Fascism and the new director of the mines. Before, there had been a Frenchman, who wanted the miners to go down the shafts wearing good shoes. In terms of shoemaking, nobody could equal Antoni Saba. They said he was a great heel and sole man, but he could make new shoes as well. He had been dead ten years and my father still wore shoes fixed by Saba. The Frenchman was a good friend of Saba's, he went to his house for dinner, and there you ate like dining in the home of a gentleman. Paté, fricassee, my father told of certain stuffed chickens whose odor alone was enough to rob the peace from a dead man, which is to say nothing of how they tasted — once you tried 'em you could never forget 'em.

Sergio Atzeni

Maybe it was '34 or '35, my memory isn't what it used to be, though I never had a good memory anyway — talking, I get lost down different side streets and back alleys...but in one of those years a new director came to Montevecchio, the first Italian director. Up till then all the directors had been French. His name was Sorbi. They said he marched on Rome and was an intimate friend of Mussolini's. Who knows whether that's true or not — Mussolini never showed his face in Guspini. The new director was there a month, no longer, when he broke all agreements with Antoni Saba. There wasn't a stuffed chicken that could convince him otherwise. That man hated anarchists. They said that in the village where he came from there had been problems with anarchists — they received beatings, were threatened....

I remember one day in May, the whole village went down to the piazza to look at the truck just arrived full of shiney new shoes made in Napoli for the commissary in Montevecchio. It was an event, shoes from the continent, in Guspini where everybody had their shoes made by Bakunin — and before him there was Bakunin's father. People used to come all the way from Arbus and Santu Ingiu to buy shoes from the Sabas. The shoes from Napoli were terrible shoes. They fell apart as soon as they got wet. The miners went to the director to protest, saying they had gotten the shaft in the deal and how! The director answered, "Maybe you're right, but this is only the first load. The next load'll be better. Or do you think that in times like these an Italian mine should be supplied with shoes from a shoemaker called Bakunin on account of his internationalist, anti-Italian loyalties? And if il Duce ever found out about it? You think I'd keep my job as director?"

So the matter was closed. The second load was worse than the first, and the third worse than the second. Those shoes literally fell apart, no kidding. It was like they were made of cardboard.

Antoni Saba fired all his workers. He had more than thirty. That July, I believe, he died. In the village they said he cut his throat with a razor. Others told how he swallowed a fistful of three-pointed nails that punctured his stomach. Daddy said he died of a broken heart, seeing his shoe factory go to pot after so much work and so many sacrifices.

Don Sarais refused to sing him mass, and didn't even want to bury him in holy ground. That way not only Bakunin's soul would be lost, but his wife's and children's too. Everyone said the suicide story was true, otherwise why would the priest have refused to bury him in holy ground?

Daddy knew that to the end Bakunin never changed his beliefs, and a few days before he died he said he wanted to be buried in the country, under a tree, with no cross nor tombstone.

7

What do you mean, of course I remember the friendship between the priest and Bakunin. Everybody talked about it. They were best of friends. The one would've risked his neck to save the other. There used to be a funny story that went around, I don't know how true it is. This is a story that I heard, which I wasn't witness to. You know how stories are, they get passed from one mouth to the next — they start out as dry little crumbs, and end up as big hot steaming loaves. People said that Saturday afternoons, when the priest, I think his name was Don Sarrabus or something like that, when he heard confessions, Bakunin

Sergio Atzeni

would crouch down behind the fountain across from the side door of the church, from where the freshly confessed women left so as not to be seen in the piazza. Many of these women stopped for a drink of water and the old man would jump out and stare straight at 'em. By the way they walked, how they drank, by the bags under their eyes, Bakunin could tell whether they'd merely confessed or actually rode the horsie in church with the priest! Word has it that later in his store — Bakunin had a shoe store I think it was, or maybe he sold carriages, or it could have been wine, it escapes me now...but in that store he used to reveal his little discoveries, and many women got beatings from their husbands because Bakunin succeeded in unmasking them. They say that he knew exactly which ones they were too, every time. It got to the point where the adulteresses who passed in front of the store would lower their eyes — they were afraid that one look from Bakunin would have betrayed 'em.

That priest there, Don Sarrastis, was a famous woman chaser. I think it was '52 or '53 when they finally kicked him out of Guspini. They turned him in to the archbishop, who sent him to Domus de Maria. That place was as near opposite its name as any place could be. House of the devil they called it, way up in the mountains, nobody there but four poachers, three fishermen, and two whores. We all knew the reason: the priest got caught with his hands up Elena Simonazzi's skirt. Man, she was hot, what a piece of ass...the wife of Dr. Sorbo or Dr. Corbo, director of the mines. She was Romagnola, from the same village as il Duce, they said. But she didn't go all the way with Don Sarrabus. Two different versions of that story exist though. One has it that she ratted on the priest after he tried to have his way with her. But she was no saint herself. She just wouldn't go with the priest. Other folks used to say that, on the contrary, she did have a thing for the priest, until one time Dr. Corvo hid in the church and saw his wife jump up on the priest's lap after having taken off her underwear. The husband beat the both of 'em. Then he went and had a little chat with the archbishop.

One thing for sure — back in those days Elena Simonazzi used to find her way into my dreams at night, nude...I won't tell you what she did though. And as it turned out, a lotta men used to dream of that woman, not just me.

8

As far as remembering goes, I remember everything, son. Scuse me if I treat you like I know you already, but I got grandsons your age, and you kids are all alike today, with your long hair and earrings.... I remember, it's just that my memory scrambles everything up. Bakunin Saba died of a broken heart on account of his eldest daughter, who then became a nun. Some fools said that she became a nun in order to convince Jesus to let her father out of hell. Nonsense. He had odd ideas, that man, but he was a good man, and our Lord forgives good men, even if they don't pray. Others maintained that she entered the sisterhood after aborting a baby by a field hand who wasn't her husband. Some say that the baby was born alive, and she killed it. The village is tiny, the people whisper and invent stories, and once those poor Sabas got themselves inside the mouths of the people, they couldn't get back out again. Bakunin must have heard those stories, and his heart couldn't stand it. So the biggest sister became a nun, the other two went to the continent to serve in the house of a big landowner, who had his villa in Pisa. There remained the youngest Saba, the only boy. What could he do? He became a miner. But not here in the village. He didn't want to mix with the villagers, maybe he didn't want to be seen reduced to the same level as the others, he who was born a gentleman. Or else the director of the Montevecchio mine didn't want him, because of animosity towards towards old Bakunin. He went to Carbonia, the boy, he'd leave on his bicycle before dawn Monday morning and return on his bike Saturday after sundown. Every Sunday he'd open his closet and take out one of his gentleman's suits from days gone by, which in the mean time had grown too short and too tight for him, and he'd stroll up and down the avenue arm in arm with his mother, Donna Margherita. She was a saint that woman. With every month that passed she grew thinner and thinner, paler and paler. They walked like aristocrats, with their heads held high. As far as ideas go, that boy was the spitting image of his father. In fact, after the war, he got himself hooked up with the communists too. During the days of fascism many miners shared those same ideas.

How's that? Don Sarais? Stories about women?

Who told you that? Don Sarais was a saint.

Sent him away? When? In '53?

By '53 Don Sarais was already a missionary in Africa. He died there, seems to me 1960. He was eaten by cannibals in the Congo.

9

My husband Ottavio and I arrived in Carbonia three months before the day il Duce came to inaugurate the city. Ottavio used to say, "The pioneers shall be rewarded." In fact, at Bacu Abis it was his squad that laid the minefields, a dangerous job, and he was subsequently promoted to foreman at Carbonia. That is, he didn't have to go down the shafts and got double the pay of an ordinary miner. Ottavio got mixed up with the black shirts not because he adhered to any of their principles — his only principles were wine and money. He joined Fascism because he wanted to be sly. He said, "You'll see who gets ahead." He got ahead. On the other hand, I lost out. While he was with the army in Africa, I stayed at my father's house in the country, with my mother and father and two sisters. I was still treated as a child even though I had two children of my own. By the time Ottavio and I moved to Carbonia, I was seven months pregnant with my third. We lived in Rosmarino, the furthest neighborhood from the market, the piazza, and the Fascist meeting house. Our house was one of the last, right on top of the hill, and I was always alone. That hill stretched from Carbonia proper to Rosmarino. From the back windows you could see the countryside, past Rosmarino. What an ugly view, yellow grass, dry shrubs. From the bedroom window I could see the Cubeddu house, right across the way. There was Mr. Cubeddu, his wife, and seven children, four boys and three girls. Father and three sons miners, they were cart pushers. Ottavio never allowed me to talk to them — little people, he said.

Those were the last houses, on the border....

The day Mussolini came, Ottavio wouldn't let me go see because I didn't own a decent dress, plus I had to nurse my third child and watch the other two while they played in the mud. I heard all the shouting in the distance, sounded like a storm was brewing.

Four days later three young men, they were just boys, really, went to live in the Cubeddus' cellar.

Every evening, after Ottavio left the mine, he went to the Fascist hall to meet his friends. On certain occassions they went

Sergio Atzeni

out in a posse to pour castor oil down the throat of some hot head. Then they'd go to the Part'e Olla tavern, get roaring drunk and sing Fascist songs. The nights they castor-oiled somebody, Ottavio came back happy and spanked me jokingly. But when he was in a bad mood, he'd leave red marks that took more than a fortnight to heal.

That, or else he'd come home loaded and drop down dead on the bed.

Some nights he thought he could get me hot, but he was too drunk, and I would just give him a handjob and he'd never know the difference.

Once in a while he'd stay at the whorehouse till morning. I spent the night alone and didn't mind a bit.

Now and then he'd whip my back with his belt.

When the three guys went to live in the Cubeddus' cellar my oldest daughter was four, had exactly the same face as her father; snot ran continuously from that kid's nose, night and day, summer and winter.

I was eighteen.

You wouldn't say so looking at me now, but back then I was so hot men stared at me with eyes popping out of their heads. If I happened to be alone, they'd whistle. The ones with more balls used to come up from behind and whisper crude little innuendos. I paid no nevermind to any of 'em. I didn't know anybody, I couldn't talk to anyone. Ottavio didn't want me to. Anyhow, I knew all those frustrated perverts thought of me when they were home humping their wives.

The three guys used to come back around dusk, usually before Ottavio had uncorked his first bottle. Come to think of it, those three were always a little tipsy themselves. All the miners had a few before hitting the hay. Perhaps all men drink, even my

Bakunin's Son

father, who was a share cropper. If he didn't have his bottle every night, he got mean as a dog. Sometimes he turned evil even when he did have his bottle, but that was rare.

Elena Cubeddu was a very good woman. She was fat, had a lot of experience in life. When our husbands were gone she used to talk to me. She told me about those three guys who lived in the cellar, sleeping on straw mattresses. They had a big pot, and had filled up half the cellar with an enormous pile of onions. Every night they put some onions in the pot and boiled 'em. Then they ate 'em. They ate nothing but bread and onions. Their names were Arturo, Tullio, and Lele.

Every evening they came up the road towards Rosmarino, singing. I could hear 'em coming. Tullio had a nice voice, kind of like Beniamino Gigli. I don't know why he didn't go around and sing at the different festivals instead of working in the mines. I remember the words to one of the songs they sang:

> *Oe no amos ne naves ne portos*
> *Ne arsenale che prima vattos.*
> *Ai, cantos feridos, cantos mortos,*
> *Cantos isperdidos, cantos mutilados.*
> *Custa fit s'allegria, sos cunfortos*
> *Ch'isperaian sos soldados nostros....*

It was a long song that told of times long ago, with characters like Tiberius, Constantine, emperors, but it was as if they spoke of Italy, il Duce, the war in Africa, of what was happening in those years. Many of the black shirts were from the continent and didn't understand the words. The Sards understood, but couldn't ban the song. In those years in Italy people often spoke of the rise and fall of Rome. How could they stop a bunch of poor miners from singing?

Sergio Atzeni

When I heard the three in chorus I went to the window to watch them. There were only a few street lamps, blowing in the wind. Up there the wind always blew. Those lamps looked like upside-down piss pots, their white enamel all chipped from the stones the village kids threw at 'em. Many of the lights were out, and the street was almost dark. I always recognized Tullio though, even from afar. He was the smallest of the three. He walked with his back perfectly straight. He wore a black, threadbare coat, always the same. On him it seemed like the cloak of a prince. The light right in front of my window was out. But all I needed was a silver moon to see Tullio as he passed under, and how I would gaze at him in wonder. He looked like a cherub, the kind they paint in the churches. His lips were thick, his black curls fell onto his shoulders, and his black eyes stared back at mine. I devoured him with my eyes, and he devoured me with his.

Ottavio came home much later. In the dark, under the sheets, he asked for my services without a word. It seemed a sin to lie with such a bad man. He was even tone deaf, you should have heard him sing "Faccetta Nera," — he had a voice like stones rattling in a tin can. If he wasn't too drunk I'd turn my back to him and let him do his business from behind, so I wouldn't have to look at his ugly face. And to my ears returned Tullio's songs, or else I remembered when I was a girl playing in the countryside, looking for rabbit tracks while I gathered daisies, or maybe playing hide-and-seek, pretending I was some rich landowner's daughter who would one day be taken away by a handsome prince on a horse.... With my husband, my body was there but my mind was far away. Yes, I dreamed of another and loathed my husband.

Bakunin's Son

I remember Lele too. He was Venetian. When he sang the Sard songs he mixed up the words, not understanding anything, laughing. He was a big baby, at least two heads taller than Tullio, with a face like a horse. I'd never seen a face so odd before. But he was as good as bread that boy. You could see his soul in his eyes, a child's soul, an innocent soul.

Every night I heard their voices, went to the window and waited. I'd be wearing my nightgown, unbottoned at the top. When the three passed below I stuck out my chest so they could get a peek, and it was white as the moon.

One night I thought, "This time I'll jump out the window, grab Tullio, and give him a kiss." Of course I didn't do it. But it was as if Tullio had read my mind, because the next night I heard only one voice, singing softly. There stood Tullio at the bottom of the hill, a tiny figure in the distance, just back from the mines. It was February, it was dark. My heart began to beat, I could hardly catch my breath. I took my place at the window.

I felt his eyes getting closer and closer, looking up at me in the window as I looked down at him. Almost without thinking I unbuttoned my nightgown a little more than usual, so he could see both my breasts, everything.

He arrived under the window, stopped, and said, "Good evening," with the voice of a child.

"How old are you?" I asked.

"Sixteen."

"No friends tonight?" I said, just to say something. I could have said anything really, and he would have stayed right where he was, watching me, with his eyes in that way.

Finally he answered, "I didn't feel like stopping at the tavern tonight."

Sergio Atzeni

I thought, "If he says he wants to make love to me, I'll say yes."

"Can I have a drink of water?" he said.

"Yes, come on up."

As he climbed the six steps that led to the door, I ran to open it like I was, with my nightgown completely unbuttoned. I don't know what had gotten into me that night. I never felt that way again, in all my life. I was walking on soft, puffy clouds. I felt like I was flying.

I opened the door. We looked at each other. Then I shook with fear, imagining that someone might see us. I closed the door.

Then I said, "No, no," because you're supposed to say no. But it meant yes. The tone of your voice counts more than your actual words.

He kissed me, keeping his eyes open. They were the color of hazelnut shells, with little specks of green, like grass in May.

From that day on, as soon as he left the mines, he came to me, not bothering to stop at the tavern. For him, I was the tavern, I was the wine, I was his dinner, his bread, his everything. No one had ever treated me the way he did, no one before and no one since. He held me like a jewel, played with me like a puppy, drank in my scent like as if from a flower.

I've never told this story to a man before. But you're different. Maybe it's because you're just a kid. Don't be offended. You seem like a kid — you're so young, I'm so old. It's nice to recall this story.

After a while, though, Tullio had to leave. His mother was sick.

I waited for him, months and months. Ottavio disgusted me. To have to touch that louse, to have to perform my services for him, to have him sleeping next to me, oh how he reeked of wine and castor oil — I could have puked on him. When he took me in his arms I cried. He used to beat me. And the more he beat me, the more I despised him.

One night Tullio came back, white as a sheet. "Let's run away," he said, "my mother is dead. I have a house. We'll live as man and wife. You can even bring your husband's kids. Come on."

We made love. It was very beautiful, more beautiful than all the other times put together — because I knew it would be the last time. I wasn't leaving with him. I didn't have the courage to go. Ottavio would have come looking for me, either him or his friends. And when he found me he would have killed me, this was certain.

After we made love, I sent him away.

He cried.

A month later the singing started up again. It was Lele.

I unbuttoned my nightgown. And Lele came through the door.

I had seventeen children. The first was a girl, same face as Ottavio. She died at the age of seven, drowned in the river. She was with her father and his friends, dove in too soon after eating.

I didn't cry.

My fourth child, a girl, was by Tullio. She's got his eyes, his curls, his mouth. Now she works in the Town Hall, in Carbonia. She doesn't know anything about this story.

The fifth child was Lele's, with a horse face just like his.

He's dead too, was only one and a half. Polio.

Four of my little ones died, plus one who was a soldier, run over by a car. Twelve are living, eight of whom are not Ottavio's, but that's the way it goes. It's a rotten thing to say now that Ottavio's dead himself. Or maybe it's not rotten at all. He died last year, cancer of the liver. May his soul rest in peace, if he has one.

10

I knew him in Carbonia. He had a lover and didn't like to work.

11

Him I don't remember. What can you do, I'm old. But the mother, sure, I remember her. When I was a girl I used to see her walking — she was the most beautiful, best-dressed woman in all the village. When she ran out of money for silk shirts, she killed herself.

12

It was a great shock, almost in one fell blow the money was gone, then her husband, and she found herself all alone in the old house. One daughter had become a nun, the other two went into service on the continent. The son stayed on the island, but worked in the mines far away. Back in the good old days many fellow villagers took advantage of her — she offered them lunches and dinners and gave them money. The Saba family was very generous, they gave to everybody without thinking twice. And when the people passed her in the street, it was,"Signora this,

Bakunin's Son

Signora that," but they were all two-faced, jealous of her, they maligned her behind her back. When bad luck came around, most of the folks wouldn't even speak to their former benefactor. When she went for her walk Sunday afternoon, they turned their heads away or high-tailed it in the opposite direction. Then, all of a sudden they started talking to her again, but friendship wasn't the motive.

The son came home every Sunday. He brought her all his pay. Many of those who used to call him a little gentleman had to eat their words. He was fifteen and had the appearance of a boy, but the heart of a man. He worked in another mine — not the shafts of Montevecchio. For him it would have been too humiliating to march with the other miners at dawn down the same streets where he used to walk dressed as a gentleman.

A few months after the wife had buried old Saba, no more, word spread that the dead man had been possessed of a certain foresight and had left some gold from the good years hidden in the garden. The greediest among the villagers began to greet Donna Margherita again, they were very obsequious. Then began the great pilgrimage: they went to visit the widow, not that they had any interest in seeing her, as you can imagine. Oh, what contrite faces they wore as they falsely mourned the passing of her husband. Coming and going they would pause in the garden and pretend to admire the almond, pomegranate, lemon, and quince trees. Really these snoopers were testing the ground with special sticks they carried. They leaned on these sticks, like they were walking sticks or canes, with the most nonchalant air, pushing down, trying to feel something. It was a beautiful garden, well cared for, fertilized, with the stones removed long ago.

Sergio Atzeni

The ground was soft, and the visitors' sticks sank down with ease — but folks left quite disillusioned. Donna Margherita didn't realize they were trying to trick her. I saw them from the window of my tailor shop and laughed to myself.

One night someone, I don't know who, climbed over the garden wall and with a pick dug up the entire garden in search of buried treasure. Next morning the place looked like it'd been run over by a herd of wild boars, ploughed and ready to be seeded. When Donna Margherita saw the mess, she laughed. It was the first time I saw her laugh since her husband died.

In the village people started saying the chest filled with gold wasn't buried in the garden, where anybody could rob it, but in the house, behind a wall.

Trying to justify their insistence on entering a house where they themselves knew the open door was merely a sign of good manners, the uninvited guests brought little gifts — hard, stale cakes or a basket of fruit, lovely on the outside, rotten on the inside. They took advantage of such occasions to knock on the walls here and there, up and down, hoping to detect a difference in sound that might indicate the whereabouts of the much-sought-after treasure. This is how I saw them....

In her first months of solitude I was Donna Margherita's only friend. I kept my respect for her like I always have. A Signora is a Signora, rich or poor that she may be. Whoever thinks that what matters is money or land doesn't know what the word Signora means. Every now and then, in the evening, she came into my shop. She sat down. Didn't speak. But I could tell she wasn't well. I asked her for advice on sizes, colors, fabrics. She had good taste, and I could see that distracting her with such insignificant things made her smile.

Bakunin's Son

One evening she came and said to me, "Maria, I'm afraid that someone's gonna break in at night. After that trouble in the garden I don't feel safe. Why don't you come and sleep at my house?" Until then I had always slept in the back room of the tailor shop. I was alone like her, about the same age. I went. In all the time I lived with her I never once heard her complain about the bad luck that had befallen her. And if she had complained she would have had all the right in the world to do so. Not like Giuditta, Totoi Zuddas' wife — now there was a woman who complained continuously about the evil of this world, always afraid that someone'd cast the old evil eye upon her and her wealth'd go down the drain. She was born a servant and reasoned like a servant. Many a fortune teller made a fortune off that witch, that's for sure.

I was there when folks came to knock on Donna Margherita's walls. They eventually lost hope having heard no sign of a hiding place for secret treasure. The real die-hards said that it must have been hidden in a closet or wardrobe, and word went round that the gold was kept in a strong box right next to our bed, out of fear that someone might steal it. Rumor had it that I was promised half the gold just to keep its whereabouts a secret. It wouldn't have surprised me to hear that I myself was plotting to poison my only friend just to get my hands on the booty.

None of the bums ever bothered to consider the fact that if Donna Margherita had really been rich, she wouldn't have sent her son off to Carbonia to break his back in the mines.

One of the women who envied Donna Margherita most used to invite the Signora to take part in the bread baking or grape harvest in the hopes that such hard work would draw a confession out of her. But she never went. She only went out on

Sergio Atzeni

Sundays. She took walks down the avenue with her son. They walked regally, even if their shoes weren't shiney and new like before.

As the months passed Donna Margherita got skinnier and skinnier, paler and paler. She ate almost nothing. In the end she was so consumed by sorrow that her dresses hung on her like sheets on a clothes line, blowing in the wind. She didn't have any flesh to hold her clothes still.

When her son saw her in such a state, he returned to the village and began working in the mine at Montevecchio. The boy and I both rose at dawn. He left for work with the other miners, heading for the shafts, while I prepared a cup of warm milk for the mother, though she hardly ever drank it.

One morning I entered the room and found Donna Margherita standing by the window, looking out. She was watching her son disappear in the distance. Tears ran down her cheeks. She turned and saw me. I didn't have the courage to say anything. She dried her tears with the back of her hand and with a sneer said to me, "There's nothing anybody can do about it, Tullio goes to the mines to feed me, but at his age he should be studying, doing something important, because he's a good boy, a handsome young man, not stupid."

A few days passed, and one morning she couldn't get out of bed. "I have a pain in my side," she said. That night she died, in silence, without disturbing anybody. I washed and dressed her, she was white as a spirit in purgatory, nothing but skin and bones. Her hair was black, black as a crow; I undid her braid; her hair was so long it touched the floor, fine and soft as silk.

She died of a broken heart. She couldn't bear seeing her son a miner, for the miners were the lowest of the low in that village

Bakunin's Son

— even some of old Totoi Zuddas' servants would have been stooping had they taken jobs in the mine.

I truly loved that woman, and still do. Sometimes I imagine I hear her footsteps, at night in the shop. And when I choose the material for a dress for one of my clients, old as I am, I can hear her voice saying, "That's nice, very fine, very elegant."

13

During Fascism I was a clerk at the Montevecchio mines. I remember that man very well. He had a big mouth, liked to stir up people. A real hot head, one of the worst. To anyone who said that he and a certain Serra, another fine element, were the best shaft-support builders around I responded, just as I would today, that if they had had families to think of and mouths to feed, well they wouldn't have worked so slow. I'm still of the idea that certain fine touches as far as mine shaft supports go are only wastes of time not worth anything. If bad luck's gonna happen, it's destiny, and you can't do anything about it. In 1944 I got a new job and moved to a different town.

14

His first days at Montevecchio he was quite the little gentleman. In part jokingly, in part to put him in his place, we told him things like, "Have you finished showing off, New Shoes?" or, "Imagine, a real dandy down in the mines, if that doesn't beat all!" You understand, just teasing, not meant to be mean or

Sergio Atzeni

anything, because none of us miners would have wished a life in the mines on anybody but our worst enemy. It was something new, Tullio Saba wearing old beat up boots like the rest of us, walking up the same road towards the shafts together with us. In those days we left for the mines early in the morning. The miners always wore something over their heads to protect them from the damp. Some wore rags, others caps. But Tullio Saba, from the first day, wore a French beret. Seemed like he did it on purpose so he would continue to stand out. Now this beret didn't go over too big with the guards and clerks at Montevecchio. Who knows why? Maybe they thought he was being arrogant and it was this they couldn't put up with. But il Duce never said it was prohibited for miners to wear French berets. In no more than a fortnight every man among us who was frustrated, who longed for a different world and who would have at least been satisfied with a new job, had got himself a hat just like Tullio's.

He lived in the center of town, I lived on the edge. In the morning I waited in the kitchen near the fireplace where it was warm, watching the street from the window. I saw him come round Angelino Marrocu's corner, down there, see? Back then there wasn't that building, only a little mud house. Angelino Marrocu was a blacksmith. When Tullio turned the corner it seemed as if he was rising out of the sparks that flew from Angelino's shop. He walked briskly to keep warm. Then I would go out and meet him here in front and we started our climb up the road together. "Ciao, Tullio." "Ciao, Ulisse." And side by side we went, without a word, each immersed in his own thoughts. Miners think a lot. Everybody whose destiny it is to carry a terrible weight on his shoulders thinks a lot. They dream of changing their lives. They think of how to free their children.

Bakunin's Son

Once in a while, after we had walked that road together for a few months, we started up a little bullshittin', in low voices. In Carbonia Tullio met miners who had been in Belgium and France. He also knew about things that weren't written in the newspapers, and what the radio didn't say, about the war in Spain and communism in Russia. He said what he knew, he told stories.

After four or five months Giacomo Serra joined us. He was older than us by at least ten years, which made him about thirty, but he seemed much older, after fifteen years working in the mines. Skinny as a bamboo shoot, back bent, his head leaning forward on his chest like a hunchback, as if his spine was too weak to be able to hold his head up straight like other people's. Maybe he'd become that way because he was always bent over down in the shafts building supports. He knew the insides of Montevecchio better than any engineer or director. Walking the tunnels, if you spotted a support built true to the rules of art, it had to be the work of Giacomo Serra. In those days there was the piecework system, so it wasn't the quality of the work that counted, but the quantity. He lost money and weeks, made enemies with the overseers, but no support of his ever burried any miner. Sometimes a well-made support isn't enough, cause if a mine wants to kill it'll break even iron. But with Giacomo Serra it was like a saint protected his work. The only support man whose work stood the test of time without a crack. He became a legend. The miners loved him. It's nice to know that there's somebody cares about rocks and water and death not crumbling on you. Few support men imitated him, although they did admire him. They had families, mouths to feed, little time to waste.

Giacomo coughed all year round, including July and August, a heavy smoker's cough. The index and middle fingers of his right hand were black with nicotine. He had black lung too.

Sergio Atzeni

He was able to get us on his squad. One day they sent us to number seven, the deepest tunnel, three-hundred-fifty meters down in the bowels of the earth. Other shafts went down as far as five-hundred meters, number ten for example, the last one. The last mine's always named after a women, like Margherita, Christina, or Elena, maybe because shafts so deep are dangerous, unfaithful, two-faced sons of bitches just like women themselves. There was a break in the pumps, a stretch of tunnel collapsed. At night, luckily. Excessive water infiltration. The support structures, poorly made, easily gave way. It was a short stretch, ten meters maybe. We took seven days to repair it. After the job was completed any miner who happened to pass through that tunnel could look up and read in letters as tall as a man: "Viva Stalin" painted on the wall.

Who was Stalin for us back then? I'm talking about the last years before the war. Who was he? He was the leader of the country without bosses, where miners earned more than engineers because they did back-breaking work in dangerous conditions; for us, Russia was a country that would have honored the work of Giacomo Serra as an example to imitate, where thrived free love, where the miners went to concerts and to the theater, in evening attire. Tullio told us these things, what reason did we have not to believe him? It was nice to imagine that somewhere in this world the first preoccupation of the government was to make sure that every miner made it out of the shafts alive. And that he didn't have to work in water up to his hips or wear fallen-apart shoes. We took for granted the truth of this news. After the war the tune changed. We began hearing about the trials of '37, how some comrades had been killed…. In the beginning we thought the ones brought to trial were traitors, then slowly we began to understand. During the years of Fascism Stalin was the good father, Benito the wicked stepfather. Now everything's changed, what we believed in back then today seems ridiculous. Even the Party says Stalin was a criminal.

You wanna know what I say? I'd give everything I have to be able to go back and feel that same way we did when we gazed upon the finished support and the shiney writing up above, "Viva Stalin."

In the months that followed we often thought of that writing which we painted with such patience down in the bowels of the earth. Neither the director nor the engineer ever went down number seven, they couldn't take it down there. But we figured that sooner or later word would spread about our grafitti, and the director and the engineer would end up going down to see it with their own eyes, and we would have gotten in trouble. Instead, nobody told them, ever.

Giacomo Serra remembered the times before Fascism. His father had been a miner too. He told us how the life of the miner was just as rotten, only back then at least the miners had a voice, they had the power to strike, the union defended the rights of the workers, and the commissary sold the best shoes and spaghetti.

We often spoke of the past, of far away people, strangers to us. We dreamed.

One day a discussion rose up: if we do like in Russia and take power, who will be put before the firing squad? Tullio said that he wouldn't shoot the director and the engineer, but would have enjoyed it much more seeing them pushing a cart and digging in the mines.

Every now and then Giacomo said that one of these days Lussu was going to disembark at Bosa — why Bosa and not Porto Torres no one knew — and give the signal for revolution. As far as I was concerned, a signal would have been all that was needed. If I had been certain that the revolution had begun I would have taken up arms and begun shooting. I would have shot the director myself.

Talk, dreams, they helped us survive.

One day Tullio showed up carrying a bunch of little sheets of red paper. On each flyer was printed a lengthy discourse in black ink that smeared all over your fingers when you touched it. It said that a new international war was about to break out and that we workers should transform it into a general revolution. After all, it pointed out, it was the miners who supplied the raw materials that fed the war industry, and therefore it was our job to sabotage production in the name of communism. We passed the flyers out only to those who for certain wouldn't give us away.

Despite that little flyer, in '39 a world war still seemed impossible to me. My father had been on Carso, came back lame. He had spoken to me of the Great War and to me it seemed quite impossible that men could be so stupid as to want to start up any such foolishness again. Then I saw with my own eyes how it was possible.

In '40 to earn what you'd earned in '39 you had to work twice as hard. Only our squad was able to maintain the pre-war slowness, but just for a time.

I've lost my train of thought, you'll have to excuse me, many years have passed....

I was talking about that little flyer we handed out, that's right, and one day the director calls Giacomo into his office. It was to tell him to get himself and his squad in gear with regard to the piecework, or else they'd all be fired. He also mentioned certain subversive little flyers, like he knew something, like he had his suspicions, without being one-hundred percent sure. That evening, heading back down to town, I said, "We'll make the supports the way he wants, they'll cave in. Don't you get it? Collapses delay production. It's sabotage. For Stalin." Giacomo Serra had this to reply: "Let a tunnel fall on a family man's head, while he's down in the bottom of a shaft earning bread for his family? Not even if Stalin came here in person to ask such a thing. Why, he couldn't be such an asshole." He didn't wanna hear any more. So for the duration of the war we broke our necks to build supports as solid as the ones before, only in more of a hurry.

At that time any celebration of May Day was prohibited, May first was just another work day. In Guspini, on their way to work on May first, the miners walked with their noses in the air, looking around, smiling. Just outside of town stood a huge mass of granite at the fork of the road, and right on top, where it's difficult to get to for anybody but a mountain goat, flew a red flag. If there was no wind the flag lay limp, but it was beautiful and red and everybody could see it all the same. Even little things like this help in times when you got to struggle ahead.

The night of April thirtieth of '41 word spread from house to house, the carabinieri are blocking the road that leads to that little granite mountain, they and the Fascist police have surrounded the whole town. No one can get out. I ran to Giacomo Serra's house. Tullio was there. So was Giacomo's sister, a little woman, ugly, always dressed in black; she feared God and priests, the complete opposite of her brother. But for Giacomo she would even take on the authorities, one against a hundred. We talked about where the best place might be to break police lines. Break police lines? More like sneak under the carabinieri's noses without getting caught. Well, it was two in the morning and we were

Sergio Atzeni

still talking trying to figure out what to do. It looked like tomorrow would be a great disappointment, our celebration would be cancelled and the Fascists would have beaten us for the first time. Then Giacomo's sister, who hadn't said a word up till that moment, said, "If the carabinieri and the Fascists are surrounding the village from the outside, we can put the flag inside the village. Not on a house, the people who live there could be persecuted. It would be too easy to get if we hung it on a light pole, they'd have it down in five minutes. The best place is on top of the church steeple. They'll never suspect Don Sarais of being a Communist." We laughed, as if she had just told a joke. Who could climb up the steeple anyway? But Tullio said, "She's right. We need some rope." Giacomo's sister disappears. Fifteen minutes later she's back with a rope twenty-meters long, stolen out of who knows what well. I told you, she was ugly, but that night I would have kissed her. I started imagining the flag flying on the steeple and the faces of the carabinieri and mayor.

It was a warm night, but cloudy, no moon nor stars. The door which led to the steeple was big and heavy, but the lock was old and encrusted, we broke it without a sound. Tullio disappeared into the dark.

We heard thunder. Then there was lightning. A very light rain began to fall, a warm mist. Giacomo and I stood completely still under the steeple looking up. Nothing moved, we couldn't see anything. Water ran from our shoes in little rivulets. We were soaked. I wanted to call out loud for Tullio, just to reassure myself, but I didn't want to attract attention. I began thinking that God was against us. I know, God is good, he's always on the side of the poor and desperate, and it'd be easier for a camel to fit through the eye of a needle than for Totoi Zuddas to get to heaven. But I was afraid, maybe I even cursed.

Bakunin's Son

I seemed to hear Giacomo's heart beating. Maybe it was my heart. My mouth was dry. I was thinking about Tullio. How was he gonna jump from the bell to the spire? Where did he tie the rope? What made him want to be the one to climb up? I thought, with both his mother and father dead, the rest of his family split up and their fortune gone.... At any moment I expected to hear a scream and see Tullio come falling down towards the ground. There were street lights, I would have seen him. Suddenly the priest's dog starts barking furiously. Maybe he'd picked up on our scents, or maybe the storm had made him nervous.

In the courtyard he kept barking and barking, scratching at the door that led to the rectory, until a window opened slowly; the lightning lit up the face of the priest wearing his woolen nightcap with pompom. He starts yelling, "What is it? Who's there? Bassino! Bassino!" Bassino was the dog's name, which in Sard means "bed pan" — that priest was a real joker all right, the kind who gets his kicks by giving an insulting name to his pet; sometimes he called Bassino the perpetual Trottrodda, which doesn't mean anything, really, just an insult. Anyway, the dog was barking his head off and the priest kept yelling, "What is it? Who is it? Strangers in the courtyard? Robbers in the streets? Cut-throats about? Help! Help!" And right as the priest's calling for help the bells start ringing as loud as they could. "He's flipped," Giacomo said to me loud enough to make himself heard over all that racket. He was referring to Tullio.

The bells kept ringing. The windows of all the houses opened. Tullio bolted out of the door of the courtyard and we ran. Everybody could hear our footsteps, but nobody recognized us, dark as it was, with all that commotion, bells ringing, thunder and lightning, the priest yelling, the carabinieri yelling too as they charged into the village.

Sergio Atzeni

For the rest of the night we didn't move from Giacomo's cellar. His sister laughed.

What happened: Tullio didn't use the rope to secure himself climbing up the spire. He climbed that part like a cat. Said he felt safer that way. Then, flag in place, he came down to where the bells were and heard the priest yelling. In order to scare the people away from coming to help the priest, Tullio tied his rope to the big bell's clapper and ran down the stairs, pulling the rope, causing the big bell to ring and strike the smaller bells around it. He ran and ran and pulled and pulled until the rope ran out, and the bells continued for a while by themselves. You think just the opposite would have happened, do you? Everybody out to help the priest when the bells ring? You don't know people. The more noise there is, the harder it is to find your pants in the dark.

You've come to me for news of Tullio Saba. The facts of that night reveal the kind of man he was: more reckless than brave, he wasn't as smart as he was crazy. If we take a minute and think about it: Why did he risk his life? May Day was just a bullshit excuse, a laugh. Well, that was our anti-Fascist movement, we were too few and too weak to do anything more. Rash acts just to see a flag flying on May Day, protest grafitti written on the walls of a mine deep below the earth, prophetic, nonsense flyers.

May Day morning, 1941, the sky was gray and blue, clean. A crowd of one hundred, made up of carabinieri and curious citizens, was gathered round the steeple. The ranks of the onlookers even included miners who had no problem giving up an hour's pay to witness the acrobatics of a certain carabiniere marshall, a terrible braggart by reputation, as he he attempted to slip and slide his way up the steeple while tied to a rope. No matter how hard he tried he just couldn't make it up. After a good hour they sent up a carabiniere private, a boy from Lucano, who climbed up that steeple like a cat, without a rope, and at last reached the top and took down the flag.

In September of '41 a piece of number six fell in. Daytime. Nine miners were trapped underneath. Eight we saved, a new fellow died, from Serrenti I think. He was seventeen years old.

Next day we gathered in the little square where management's offices were. I don't know what we really wanted. The director came to the window and spoke to us. In his eulogy of the victim he spoke of destiny. We started to laugh and yell at him. Then he changed his tone, those responsible for the death would be discovered he said, and the guilty punished. He finished amidst whistles and boos. He was the guilty one. He and the whole regime. Would the director call Benito Mussolini to trial because he had led us into war? Or would he have persecuted himself for having instituted the piecework system?

A week later he fired the entire squad responsible for building the supports for tunnel six. Making a mockery of justice, he put seven people out on the street, two of whom were the breadwinners of big families, two others newlyweds — yes, even in those years people got married, despite everything.

One evening I asked Tullio, "Still think we shouldn't kill the director?"

He didn't answer.

In 1942 Tullio left for the war, we had to work to fill his place too, even though there was one less among us, we still had to produce the same as before.

I'll stop here.

I still saw him, after the war, but I don't much feel like getting into those stories. There was the incident, the trial.... Ask somebody else. I wouldn't be objective, I myself was indicted,

Sergio Atzeni

and for a while I thought the judge would find me guilty. If you want, I'll tell you the judge's name.

15

It's easy to invent legends. Leave home and go far away. When you come back everyone'll say, "He slayed the dragon!" "He played soccer for Benfica!" "He bought a car!" "In Germany he had four women," and other stories of the kind. If you didn't actually see any of it, what can you do? Today the story about Benfica can be torn to shreds in a minute, but back in '47 who had a television? That's how it went with Tullio Saba, they called him a war hero. According to some folks it seems that Tullio liberated Italy single-handedly. It was said that he belonged to an elite battalion of saboteurs that socked it to the Nazis the way Bertoldo gave it to 'em in France.

Communist propaganda. They know what they're doing, those Communists, when it comes to propaganda...but to hear them back then you would have thought Joe Stalin was San Francesco's good brother, and many people believed it.

But do you wanna know the truth? I, in person, with my own eyes, saw Tullio Saba three times in Napoli during the war, all three times in the Spanish quarters. Soldier? Bullshit, to put it mildly. He sleazed around like an American, was mixed up in some intrigue with the family of a prostitute who towered over him by at least twenty centimeters. He lived with them in their cellar apartment located in an alley that the American officers had nicknamed "Gomorra," the name says it all.

Hero? He had some Neapolitan friends, like I said, and some American friends too, mostly blacks. Well, as they say, animals

Bakunin's Son

understand each other. One thing's for sure, the last thing on their minds was Germans. They had an accomplice in Via Toledo. A camorrista, I don't know who, Gennaro or something like that. Now I say this having heard it from utterly reliable sources. They told me all about what that risen Lazarus, that cleaned-up louse, was up to. And to think, I'd met him starving at the bottom of a coal mine in Carbonia, here he was in Naples strutting around like a sultan.

Their accomplice bought from them, then sold on the black market. Military stuff, you understand. Like shoes, and not surprisingly — you should have seen the shoes he came to the mines in, shoes that even I couldn't afford to buy, and as foreman I earned four times as much as him. Cigarettes too, also nothing to marvel at, anybody who knew him like I knew him never saw him without a cigarette in his mouth. Ah, and don't forget the bootleg booze — back home in Carbonia he was always drunk and bothering women, blaming his escapades on the booze…sly devil, that rascal…. But you, if you want my opinion, and even if you don't I'm going to give it to you anyway seeing as you asked me, why do you want to dig up that man's past? Wouldn't it be better to leave it burried? You know what happens when you stir up shit? I think you do, I mean you seem intelligent enough. Write about whorehouses, beautiful women, the codes of honor within the hierarchies, and write about happy people if you want to write a story about Fascism, because believe me, it'll be worth more. Plus it'd be the truth, in those years in Italy, apart from a few shitheads, we were all Fascists, and we did just fine. The war was a lurid infiltration of Americans, whores, niggers, and Italian traitors like Saba. And if you do make the intelligent choice like I'm suggesting, leave out the garbage, especially when it comes to Tullio Saba, who was nothing but an ignorant slob. Take it from someone who knew him personally. And while you're at it, get rid of that earring too. Don't be offended, bud. I know it's none of my business, but it's depressing seeing all you young fellows wearing earrings! What are we coming to?

16

I saw his silver medal and the parchment they gave him with my own eyes. He unrolled the parchment and showed me, it was written in English. Signed by a general, quite famous at that time, but his name escapes me now. It's on the tip of my tongue...Alexander. I could be wrong. My memory's gotten worse with the years. I think it was Alexander, but I wouldn't swear on it. A friend of mine's got a history of the Second World War at his house, I can check it for you.

The name written on the parchment was Tullio Saba. About the Americans I can tell you this: they might give away cigarettes and dollars, but medals they do not just give away, not even to American soldiers, much less Italians. You got to earn your medals. And back then this was truer than ever, but even today. Too bad I didn't understand English.

17

In the third chapel on the right there's a crying Madonna dressed in black. From the type of skirt and bodice she's wearing, and also from her chubby cheeks, more than a real Madonna she

Bakunin's Son

looks like a baker lady from around here, like maybe from Mogoro or Ales. But the expression on her face is of real pain, not like certain Madonnas I've seen, who in their despair are smiling on the sly, or looking off into the distance thinking about their own problems, or even laughing as if they were enjoying the whole thing. The Madonna in black is crying, somebody really made her suffer. This image's stuck with me ever since I was a kid. Whenever I think of someone sincerely crying, of an expression truly pained, I think of that Madonna.

One night I have this dream. The Madonna in black appears, just like she is in the chapel, wearing the same clothes, same face, but alive, not painted, and she's coming towards me. Then she speaks. "Tomorrow another innocent one shall die. That's why I'm crying. He's guilty for what he's done, but his soul is innocent. A man whose head is full of ghosts, who doesn't deserve death. A sinner, like all of you. He will be killed, that's why I'm crying."

That's what she said. Then she disappeared.

I woke up and went to work. Then in the little square in front of the mine company's offices I went to protest together with everybody else.

Somebody shot the director.

I didn't see who it was.

I saw the director with his face in the mud, his hair all dirty and wet, lying on the ground, blood running and flowing into the puddles and into the earth.

Then I was called to testify and I told everything I knew, which amounted to that dream I'd had and not much else.

Sergio Atzeni

18

I was in the little square when the director was killed. I didn't see who shot him. There was too much confusion, shouting and noise, both before and after the shooting. Someone said to me, "They've shot the director." I don't know who it was that told me. But right then I didn't realize he was dead. No. I thought he was just wounded. Then someone said, "The director's dead." I don't know who it was that told me. It was raining that morning, the little square was one big mud puddle. So who killed the director? No one ever found out. Someone said it was a vendetta for the death back in '41. Bullshit. That man didn't have relatives in the mines. Somebody said it was Allicchinu, the cuckold clerk. At first it didn't seem possible, he was such a kind, gentle man, wouldn't hurt a fly. But then again, look around, it's precisely those quiet, passive types that explode when the right moment comes along. Who knows?

19

It was winter, between the end of 1950 and the beginning of '51. The sky was continuously gray. Torrential rains. And the cold, the courtroom was like ice. Only on the day of the ruling did a timid sun manage to peep out of the clouds.

The story goes back to March of '47. The facts were at once quite clear, yet obscure, comprehensible yet hidden. The

Bakunin's Son

director of the Montevecchio shafts, a mining engineer from the Pertusola Company by the name of Sorbi, had been killed in a dirty, sad little square, where trapsing through the blackish-gray mud we carried out a thorough on-the-scenes investigation. The man had been killed in the presence of 430 witnesses. They found him lying on his back, in the mud, across from the mine's offices, which were located in a pale yellow building. Three bullets, one in his side, one in his chest, one in his neck. Shot from a pistol, I forget the make, but one thing for sure, the weapon was American, from the American arsenal. One of their officers testified to this. I didn't consider relevant the position the corpse was found in, being certain that the body had been dragged around in the mud before the carabinieri arrived. According to their report the corpse was in such a state that.... Like it had taken a bath in that mud.

The investigation was quite detailed, but we were stuck for lack of evidence. I had no doubt that the guilty party was among the three suspects charged. Which one, that was the problem. Where was the evidence? You can't base a judgment of this type only on your intuition. A man by the name of Serra, Giacomo Serra it seems to me, was thought to be the most likely. In their testimony to the carabinieri, two witnesses identified Serra as the gunman. But there was also evidence that pointed to the man you're interested in, as well as to another whose first and last names I remember perfectly, Ulisse Ardau. There was a strong suspicion that Saba had been the owner of the weapon.

From the beginning of the trial I had the unpleasant sensation that the defendants, witnesses, and even the public, which was made up of mostly miners and their relatives, all knew exactly who had shot the director. But when it came down to it nobody would talk.

Sergio Atzeni

I had the impression that every clue had been manipulated in such a way as to draw attention away from the killer. It was as if the guilty party had committed an act which the community around him approved of, or worse, had executed a sentence handed down by the people, a sort of collective judgment. As you perhaps know, in the past complex social interactions generically known as outlawry were solidified by the code of honor. Looking from the outside, many times you can only be guided by your intuition, concrete proof being quite rare. They have their own system of justice. Different groups vie for control within the closed reality of the country folk. Those who betray the common good are punished. But we don't know the intricacies of such judgments, we cannot know the real motives. All this happens in spite of the laws laid down by the governing authorities. From the outside we can observe homicides as signs of the presence of an outlaw system, but we are at pains to truly comprehend that system. Surely, there exists a certain logic behind such actions, a popular mentality that, perhaps you already know, is a tightly sealed mystery.

I don't recall which elements first fired my suspicions that the entire episode was an orchestrated deception, but it was certainly an impression which lasted throughout the trial.

Numerous witnesses testified having heard shots from the right, that is, from the direction of the tennis courts reserved for the mine management and their families. Others swore they saw a flash come from the left, from one of the windows of the office building, where approximately ten clerks were gathered, looking out. However, the majority of witness stated that they neither saw nor heard a thing.

The two witnesses whose testimony formed the basis of the case against Serra withdrew their statements, claiming they had

Bakunin's Son

been tricked by the carabinieri into giving inaccurate accounts. All they would swear to was having heard second-hand that Serra was the gunman, but they couldn't remember who they'd heard it from. I told them to go and take some time to think about it, but when they returned after four days I saw it was useless.

This was the general behavior of all those who'd originally given statements which pointed at Serra, Ardau, and Saba the alleged perpetrators of the crime. When it came to testifying in court, witnesses could not say with certainty what they had seen or where they had heard such and such information from.

Serra was calm, in complete control of himself. Every so often he even ventured to make a little joke. But he was polite, courteous, at ease. Saba came into court dressed like a provincial dandy, wearing eccentric suits, loud colors, quite a vulgar appearance. He denied every allegation. As far as the pistol went, he denied ever having owned one as a civilian. And no one admitted ever having seen him with a pistol in his hands. The third defendant, Ulisse Ardau, was nervous, trembling and sweating. Out of the blue I asked him why he was shaking. He responded that it was cold in the courtroom, which was the truth.

One witness, a miner, claimed to have been forewarned of the killing in a dream, in which there appeared the Madonna. But at the moment the shots were fired, despite his forewarning he was looking the other way or talking to someone, and neither saw nor heard a thing.

There were even stranger testimonies, really extravagant. A local haberdasher asked to testify. He claimed that an old witch of the village had met the victim in a dream, and that the victim revealed the killer's name to her. I've never believed in the existence of spirits of the dead or the possibility of communication between the world of the living and the world of the dead, not

Sergio Atzeni

before the trial and certainly not after the trial. I had the old woman called before the court because it seemed to be the collective will of the people that she testify. Was the old woman hiding something, maybe some link of kinship or other type of relationship with the killer? Perhaps the excess of conflicting evidence might betray the community, sooner or later forcing an error in the testimony of witnesses overconfident with regard to the infallibility of their collective hoax. I decided to give them enough rope to hang themselves with. The old women appeared in court. She was a little dried up old thing in a dress black as coal. She had a long, hooked nose, her tiny black eyes were lively and alert. She spoke only in Sard dialect, claimed that she couldn't speak Italian. From the first I suspected her of lying.

Under oath she declared that the victim had visited her in a dream, and that he had revealed to her the name of the killer. I asked her to specify whether it was in a dream or in a trance. She repeated that it had been a dream, adding that a judge should not take seriously the peasants' idle chatter about witchcraft, seances, and similar stories since witches do not exist, only fools believe in them, and seances are merely tricks to pull the wool over the eyes of the ignorant, and that if any villager had spoken of her as a witch, well, consider the source, those stupid folk don't even know how to speak Italian.

I asked her the name revealed by the victim. She named a clerk of the mine, one of the men who said he was looking out one of the windows where the flash had allegedly come from.

The clerk was called to the stand. He swore that, yes, he had been looking out the window when the director was killed, but he hadn't seen anything because at that moment he was looking in the direction of the tennis courts, where his wife was playing tennis. The public started to laugh. The poor man blushed. He

Bakunin's Son

admitted suspecting his wife was cheating on him, though he had as yet no concrete proof. He said the woman in question was by nature hot-tempered. He also said that he had no suspicions of any clandestine relationship between her and the director. And even if he had had such a suspicion, he wouldn't have shot the director, since he had refrained from shooting earlier suspects. He had never held a gun in his hand, he said, he didn't know how to shoot one. He spoke of his own volition, having been asked but one question at the beginning. He stuttered slightly, perspired, looked around him as if he were a hare caught in a trap. He spoke while the public egged him on, laughing and commenting under their breath. I felt sorry for the guy. That old woman had been very smart. Her testimony was a clear sign that the collective will of the people was able to make up stories, lie, obliterate the truth by creating an infallible fraud.

If I could have judged the case based on my feelings, I would have found Ardau guilty of murder and would have named the entire village his accomplice.

But no one ever said, either during the pre-trial hearing or during the trial itself, that they had seen Ardau fire the shots.

All three suspects were acquitted. The district attorney's appeal was unsuccessful.

20

I was the one who fired Saba, in April 1951, I recall every detail perfectly, I've always had a sharp memory. It marked a turning point in my life. Thanks to victory at the Montevecchio mines Mineco offered me the position of director of their operations in Bolivia.

Sergio Atzeni

Firing Saba was not, as the fools at that time said, a form of retaliation for the murder of my predecessor, the director of the mine. In April Saba was not yet accused of aiding and abetting the murder, although thanks to the carabinieri I found out that he was among the suspects. In the months after the murder his name had come up several times, along with the others who were eventually indicted. I had no intentions of taking the law into my own hands, nor could I judge a man who was yet to be tried before the court.

In order to best understand my story modern listeners must make an effort to imagine the atmosphere that dominated our country in those years: there was the widely held belief that the Communists were preparing for a great revolution, a notion held by the Communists themselves. Thus with regard to industrial relations Italy was a cauldron boiling over.

The management at Pertusola called me in because they knew my character: I was decidedly and actively anti-Communist, on the attack rather than on the defensive. In those years I voted in favor of the monarchy, while at the same time maintaining my Fascist sympathies. Why deny it? Fascist Italy wasn't the horrible place described by the Communists, and the best, most sensible historians of today recognize this fact. As far as the monarchy is concerned, if someone were to ask for my opinion, the constitutional monarchy as practiced in Great Britain would be much better for Italy than the current corrupt multi-party system.

Getting back to the point. I was twenty-seven years old when I arrived at Montevecchio. "Don't take it so hard," I'd been told, and right off the bat I could see why. The climate down there couldn't have been worse, and I don't mean the weather, but the climate in the company: the miners were convinced that

Bakunin's Son

they were the ones running the mine. They thought I would be afraid of them after the murder of my predecessor. I knew that given the opportunity, they would have knocked me off too. Of this I was certain. But I had decided to do my duty to the fullest and put things back in order as best I could.

Production in 1946-47 had fallen 80 percent with respect to the mines' output during the years 1940-41. Even taking into account factors such as the differences between the war economy of a bellicose nation and a post-war economy of a defeated one, the decline in productivity was exaggerated, especially at a time when the market tended towards upswing and prices were rising.

I was able to get a clear picture of the situation after my first week: causes of the decline in production were the strikes against the piecework system and other union-style tactics like organized late arrivals on the job; actual sabotoge of production; and psychological intimidation of management on the part of labor; besides the rest of their antics which served to throw a monkey wrench in the company hierarchy, as well as a certain congenital form of stupidity among the locals. No offense, if you're from down there, I mean. It's hard to find an intelligent man in Marmilla. The place is full of drunkards and scallywags, but people with brains....

It was an extremely arduous clash. Month after month they organized strikes. I responded with written communiqués which were posted on walls all over town. I refused to meet their representatives in person until working order was restored in the company. I didn't want them using my words to bolster their propaganda. And out of principle I don't like having the weak hand and being forced to submit to the opposition's demands in negotiations.

Sergio Atzeni

After I had been down there four months I posted a bulletin which threatened the immediate firing of all who did not show up for work the next day. For that day another strike had already been announced. The workers occupied the shafts, closed the tunnels. Their wives came to my office asking to speak to me. They appeared to be possessed. But since they themselves were not employees of the company, I refused to meet with them. They encircled the building. I called the carabinieri, who escorted me to safety in their van amidst a barrage of insults and stones hurled by the incensed mob.

I went to live at the carabinieri barracks. I became friends with one of the marshalls, a certain Piseddu, excellent card player. Hours upon hours we played cards, which relaxed me. The days went by, the storekeepers began cutting the miners' wives' credit. Every day at dawn the women walked towards the mines with baskets on their heads. And every day those baskets were less and less full, while the women's backs were more and more bent. I began feeling that victory was near.

After forty-three days the miners finally gave up and left the shafts. I saw them walk back to the village, dissolute, in a long black line with their wives at their sides. I felt sorry for both the men and their wives. But they alone, on account of their foolishness, were responsible for their destiny. I was only doing my job, and I tried to do it as best I knew how. Those poor women, staring furiously in the direction of the barracks, trying to look me in the eye as I stood at the window watching their sad parade. If their eyes could have shot poison arrows, they would have killed me. Ugly women in Marmilla, short, all hairy, with moustaches. Not to mention mean and cheating.

Bakunin's Son

I went back to Montevecchio and found the offices in awful condition. Let me just give you two examples which confirm without a doubt the idiocy of people. On my desk I kept a photo of my wife; throughout my duration as director of the Montevecchio mines I preferred to have her live in Cagliari. That picture was my daily link with her. Two days after my return to the office I found that picture in a corner of the bathroom, buried under a mountain of excrements. As far as the personal records of each employee were concerned, I found them in a pile in the square outside, burned and mutilated; you could see where the perpetrators had tried to rub out certain parts with erasers. The personnel clerks, among the most loyal of all the mine's employees hired by my predecessor, were able to reconstruct each file as it had been before the occupation. I was not the least bit disheartened by such a show of rebellion. On the contrary. If that was the best they could do, the game was already won.

I composed the text of an agreement with the miners in one night. As usual I had it posted in town. Anyone who wished to come back to work had to sign a contract. A signature meant the signer would abide whole-heartedly by the regulations set forth in the contract: the abolition of the present workers' coalition; a ban on the reformation of any union or union-type organization whatsoever; a ban on the formation of political organizations among the workers; the promise to discuss with me personally any individual gripe or problem. My plan also recognized and rewarded hard work by offering to double the salary of those workers responsible for the highest production. There were also various clauses regarding the decent behavior and personal hygiene of the workers. Too bad I didn't save that text, I'd show it to you. I'm still proud of it today. Fact is, you've got to be pitiless

Sergio Atzeni

and tough when it comes to dealing with Communists and other hot-heads, but you've also got to be smart, able to use wage incentives that create divisions among the workers, while you wield a rhetoric capable of disarming the ignorant.

I got what I wanted. A few of them held out and refused to sign, among whom that Serra who was later accused of shooting my predecessor. I communicated their names to all the mines in Sardinia, so that my colleagues would know exactly what type of clowns would be going around begging for work.

Immediately afterward I found out that the core of their subversive internal organization was still more or less intact. This was the beginning of the most perplexing period. It was more and more difficult to prevent and punish acts of sabotage. The perpetrators went into hiding. They acted only when conditions guaranteed them absolute security, so they could be sure that I would be left with no evidence to pin them with. Nonetheless we had our first increase in production, the year after the new agreement had been stipulated; sales went up a good 30 percent and we built up our stockpile. One group of workers began setting an example, though I want to emphasize that I wasn't asking them to perform absurd feats of labor worthy of Stakanov, we weren't in Russia. I showed that management didn't begrudge raises and promotions to those who deserved them. I rewarded the hard-working as I began to investigate further and further into the situation, asking lots of people lots of questions. I found things out. It was like a police investigation. Or the scientific study done in preparation for dredging and cleaning up a swamp. In the end I had a clear picture of the situation. At the center of the subversive network was one man, the brains of the operation. And this was Saba, the man you were asking about. Around him ten or so hand-picked, trustworthy henchmen, among whom

Bakunin's Son

Ardau, another one indicted in the case of my predecessor's murder. They were all backed up by a hundred loyal Communists, who were unable to produce a leader of their own.

I set up elections for a new internal commission. I presented a list of candidates that I called "Workers United." On it I even included three life-long Communists, hard and dedicated workers all the same. They hesitated, they wavered, but they didn't have the courage to refuse.

The rest of the Communists presented their own list, in opposition to mine, known as the "Free Workers." Saba was at the head of the list. He and the nine below him were all members of the CGIL — the General Italian Confederation of Workers. I could have easily considered the presentation of their list a breaching of the return-to-work pact, since such an act constituted an attempt at reconstructing a union-sponsored organization, an act the workers' contract prohibited.

The voting went off on schedule and the "Free Workers" list won 60-40. Such a showing was, in my opinion, a success, a sign that the enemy had been split up and 40 percent had been lured over to our side. All that was left to do was get rid of our adversary's ring leaders, and the battle would be considered won.

I called Saba in to talk. I'd already written up his pink slip on the grounds of breach of contract. But to tell you the truth, I still hadn't decided whether to fire him or not when Saba walked through my door. Everyone said he was an intelligent man and an expert craftsman. If only he hadn't been so pig-headed and accepted the new situation with a willingness to collaborate, I would have kept him on. I didn't want to keep him from being a Communist, nor could I have demanded he give up his beliefs. He just had to relegate Communism to his free time, that's all, leave it in the bar, and stop sabotaging production.

Sergio Atzeni

I asked him to sit down. He wouldn't sit down.

I tried to reason with him calmly, I don't remember my exact words, but they were clear, in line with what I've been explaining to you. After a few minutes he interrupted me saying I could stop right there and give him his pink slip.

He was arrogant and impolite. I gave him his pink slip without a word. He looked at me with a brazen air and pulled out a stinking Alfa cigarette which he lit right under my nose before turning around and walking out the door. With that beret on his head he could have passed for a mini Jean Gabin.

I fired all those whose names had appeared on the alternative list. I couldn't keep them on with Saba giving them orders from the outside.

I never saw him again. That meeting had taken place exactly two years after I had arrived at Montevecchio. The year after, production rose 60 percent.

21

I heard him once, in 1951 I think, when he sang with Cesarino Cappelluti. He just had a big head, he couldn't really sing.

22

The guy from Guspini who sang with Cappelluti after the war? A fashion plate, a dandy. I wouldn't know what else to say about him. Not that Gonnos is far from Guspini, it's not, but back in those days I didn't go to Guspini much, and now I go there even less. Will what I say be written in the newspaper? In a book? Well you listen to me: folks from Guspini are almost as evil and nasty as people from Villacrido, now they're really what I call down home folks — known for killing their brothers, they are. Common knowledge.

23

My sister was in love with him. He was courting Edvige Zuddas at the time. My sister eventually married the man she's married to. Terrible man. I wouldn't take a man like that even if I were dead. He ruined my sister's life. I've never met a more suspicious, critical, negative man than my brother-in-law. Jealous, quick with his fists, ugly as a dog and evil as the plague.

Tullio Saba never married Edvige and ended up leaving town. Any more than that I don't know.

But what are you still doing standing in the door? Come on in and I'll make some coffee.

24

They were strange years. There was no work, people were starving and yet they wanted to sing and dance because the war was over. In Marmilla some had danced up till '41, rich folks with a phonograph in the house, they danced in secret. But by the end of '41 till the end of the war, nobody danced. Sad years for a young man who wanted to become a musician. I played the guitar, never really as a professional, though I wasn't what you'd call a complete spaz either, just an average guitarist, the only kind that a place like Marmilla could ever produce. Marmilla really isn't known for its musicians like Santa Giusta is. Right after the war Cesarino Cappelluti took me under his wing.

Sergio Atzeni

Cesarino Cappelluti was the son of the first man to ever put a label on a bottle of Marmillese olive oil: "Cappelluti, Genuine Olive Oil Produced by Sir Arturo Cappelluti. Made in Gonnosfanadiga, Kingdom of Sardinia, Italy, and Jerusalem." Arturo Cappelluti had advertisements for his oil printed up and hung 'em on the walls of the town squares of every village within a day's ride of Marmilla, back in the 1920s. I was just a boy, but I remember the scandal. What laughter arose when people got a load of those posters! For years thereafter my father would go around repeating the slogan that appeared at the top of those posters, chuckling, "Use Cappelluti in the kitchen and you'll never suffer from distemper."

Nobody ever bought the olive oil bottled by Cappelluti. Every family in those parts had their own supply of olives, either because they owned a piece of land with olive trees on it or were paid in kind for harvesting others' olives. People brought their olives to the village olive press and everyone made their own oil. The situation was exactly the same in all the surrounding villages — olives and olive presses, that's olive country, boy. Nobody would even consider buying olive oil off some city-slicker just arrived from the continent, let alone off some jerk who went around putting up posters all over the place.

Arturo Cappelluti was a legend, a failure, but a legend. He ended up selling his entire stock of olive oil to a merchant from Cagliari for a crust of bread. He turned his store into a house and went to earn his living in the fields. He wasn't a knight.

No one ever understood why a man who for thirty-four years had lived in Ostiglia, working in the post office, would ever decide to come and make it big in a place like Marmilla. Not that it's impossible to see why anyone would want to leave Ostiglia,

Bakunin's Son

more than likely a hole in the wall itself, I don't know, I've never been there. The old folks used to say, "You wanna escape Ostiglia, go to Mantova or Milano, they're just around the corner. Only a fool would come to Marmilla."

Cesarino never talked about his father's flight to Sardinia. Maybe he never knew anything about it, maybe he was never told. Or maybe he kept silent out of respect for the father. As far as I know, Cesarino never set foot in Ostiglia and never knew his mother.

Cesarino was a skinny accordian player, to my knowledge the only person from Marmilla ever to earn a living as a musician his whole life long. He wasn't born in Marmilla. He came when he was two, but he grew up like he was one of us, spoke better Sard than he did Italian. Leader of the band since he was eighteen. In thirty years he founded and broke up many different bands, maybe you've heard of some: The Bingo Band, Cesarino Cappelluti and His Orchestra, New Poverty, SuperMozart, The Blue Falcons, The Last Beach, Navajos, Marmilla Supersound Band. Now he's leading The Jujus. They're not famous in Marmilla. He's sixty-four years old, no kid. He even played abroad once, on the cruise ship *Achille Lauro*. He's played on the continent six or seven times, and one time was even on TV — but no one on the continent watched and no one in Marmilla had a TV then.

He picked me up right after the war and we played at weddings and religious festivals together.

He played the accordian and I accompanied him on the guitar and sang. In 1950 we did the wedding of a very rich fellow in Tuili, paid us in real money too — not like everyone else, who gave us chickens, sugar, coffee. Our pockets full of coins, jingling,

Sergio Atzeni

Cesarino said, "Let's go to Cagliari, I want to buy me a trumpet and learn how to play."

We got off the train, it was a nice sunny day, and under the porticoes across from the port, there was a crowd of beautiful girls milling about; we walked with our eyes popping out of our heads, we felt light on our feet, like in a dream. Back in those days Cagliari had that effect on me. But no more. Passing under the porticoes we heard a clarinet from one of the alleys. We followed the sound to see who was playing. Among the ruins of a house that must have been bombed back in '43 at least a hundred people were dancing under the hot sun. A six-foot tall black man in an American military shirt with the stripes torn off was leaned up against the remains of a yellow wall, blowing his clarinet like a madman. He was probably with the corps that sprayed DDT to get rid of the malaria. At his side was a little Chinaman, a midget compared to the blackman, also in American military dress, keeping the beat on some old tin cans. The Chinaman didn't stop smiling, whereas the black man gazed over the people's heads, towards the sea, with red eyes, a lost look on his face. Cesarino listened for a while. Then grabbed his accordian, which he always brought along wherever he went, and started jamming with 'em.

Later on they continued their jam session in a tavern.

Afterwards we went to Sant'Elia. Back in those days there weren't even houses at Sant'Elia, much less a stadium, only grass, rocks, bushes, and the sea and the sea air. I don't exactly remember what happened, I was drunk on wine and music. I woke up on the beach…Cesarino and the Chinaman were awake, sitting side by side in the sand, looking out at the sea, singing a sweet song, almost in a whisper. The black guy was still asleep,

Bakunin's Son

two girls with long braids sleeping with him, their heads on his chest — all three smiling as they slept.

At ten that morning the soldiers shipped out. If I had played like Cesarino I would have shipped out too and followed them to the USA. But I wasn't so hot and Cesarino wouldn't even think of it. Strange bunch, those Cappellutis — the father wound up in Marmilla like I said, and the son who never left the island except for a few short trips to Italy and a forty-day cruise on the *Achille Lauro*.

Oh yeah, Cesarino bought that trumpet — ten years later.

But getting back to the story...at that time we played all over Marmilla, except Guspini. This was due to the fact that both Cesarino and I were from Gonnos. Just as people from Gonnos would never call anyone from Guspini to play at their wedding, no one from Guspini would hire musicians from Gonnos. That's how it was, a certain mistrust passed through the generations, from father to son. But one day, in early 1951, someone from Guspini called us to do a wedding. I didn't like the idea, and it was clear that the guy who called us had something against the people of his own village and wanted to demonstrate this publically by hiring musicians from Gonnos. There could be trouble. The guy who called 's name was Ulysses. In Guspini there are all kinds of people, just like everywhere else, but especially stubborn, evil people, and the guy who called was typical, blessed with both these traits. Cesarino couldn't hold himself back when the crazies called — he wanted to be right in the thick of all the madness. He was the bandleader, so we headed for Guspini, and there, for the first time, I had the pleasure of meeting Tullio Saba, the one you asked me about.

I picked him out in church. He was dressed as an American soldier, smiling at everybody with a kind of mocking sneer. And

Sergio Atzeni

during the reception he started cracking dirty jokes and singing little limericks about what awaited the newlyweds on their first night together. He wouldn't shut up. After the dinner we played and he joined us — he sang. He had a light tenor voice, nothing great. Then, together with some of the guests — we were all a bit drunk — we hit a nearby tavern, where Cesarino went into the songs he'd learned from that black soldier — and that's how we found out that Tullio Saba knew the words to all of 'em. There Tullio won Cesarino over completely — if Saba's craziness hadn't already been enough for him.

He joined the orchestra. Cesarino and I went to live with him in his house in Guspini.

As singer for a wedding band, Tullio Saba was a disaster. What a voice — half the week he couldn't sing at all, and the other half he squeaked his high notes so that the whole thing became a joke. Then he'd inevitably start in on the wisecracks, making fun of the married couple, which tended to irritate the bridegroom and his friends. Sometimes fights broke out. He also riled the guests by the way he dressed, trying to imitate some American actor whose name escapes me just now.... At night, after the wedding receptions, we'd get drinking, and Cesarino tore into those American songs. Tullio sang alright, but not like he sang the wedding songs. The night would do something to his voice, it completely changed, sent shivers down your spine — that voice became irresistible, I don't know why. There was one song, I'd still like to hear him sing it today, that went, "Me and my gin...." You could tell that was the song for him.

We met Tullio in early 1951, and in April he fell in love with a girl from his village, a love which eventually led the orchestra to destruction. It's a story that changed my life. The girl's name was Edvige. I tried to talk him out of it, I knew the whole thing was gonna bring us bad luck. From the beginning his passion for Edvige had adverse effects on the band. We had a string of gigs lined up all over Marmilla, but he didn't want to leave Guspini. I used to say to him, "How can you say, 'I love you Edvige,' and keep a straight face? With a name like that...." But then one day I saw her on the street and said to myself, "God, what a beast, how can Tullio even bear to look at her?" She was nearly six-feet tall, a cow. From the beginning this was a love affair tinged with masochism on Tullio's part, which I never understood, though in the end I could sort of guess why.

Every night we serenaded Edvige.

At home there was always fresh bread, cheese, and wine. Besides us three, no one ever came into the house that I knew of. Tullio was always with us. At night we'd go sing under Edvige's window, we'd get back home very late. It'd be noon before we got up, and when we went down to the kitchen we'd find fresh bread, a piece of cheese, and two big bottles of wine on the table. Who brought it? I never really asked myself where that food came from: at that time all we could think of was how to get Tullio away from that girl. But now, after all these years, the one thing that still gnaws at my curiosity is the mystery of that food — I can't figure out who used to bring it. And why did they bring it? Tullio never said a word about it. To him it seemed the most normal thing in the world, that there should be food on the table for us when we got up.

After three or four serenades even Cesarino changed, like he was hot for Edvige too, and played for her like he played for no one else, not before, not since, an Orpheus, with an intense passion.

It must have been a hundred years since anybody serenaded a girl in Guspini. A few old people said they remembered a time

Sergio Atzeni

when serenades were fashionable, others denied it. But even if it had been a hundred years since the last serenades, most everybody seemed to enjoy ours. Word spread quickly and young men all over, even as far as Seddori and Santu Ingiu, started serenading their girls.

One night, going down the street that led to Edvige's window, we met up with a gang of ten guys, by the looks of whom were field hands. They lined up and blocked the road. One stepped out in front and said, "La Signora Edvige has a fiancé and 's engaged to be married. Go and serenade someone else."

All I could think was, "Only in Guspini would men make such a big deal over a monster like Edvige."

"Engaged to who?" asked Tullio.

"None of your business to who," said the speaker of the group.

"To one of you?" asked Tullio, and getting no response, he continued, "If it is one of you, why didn't you wait for me alone, so we could talk this thing out man to man? Why do you need all these bodyguards? Are you chicken? What kind of man are you?"

No one answered, and the madman started in again, "So he's not with you. He sent you guys here. He's afraid to show himself in the street, even with ten bodyguards. How much is he paying you? Is he buying you dinner too? Is he rich?"

"Put a lid on it, red," said the speaker.

"What does red or black or whatever have to do with any of this? I'm in love with Edvige. She's not married. And even if she was married, tough luck for her husband. If she comes to the window and tells me to go, I'll leave. If she doesn't tell me to go, I'll keep singing in honor of her beauty. Is your boss in love with her like I am? Tell him to come and serenade her."

Bakunin's Son

It seemed like Tullio was only in love with foolishness, and ready for anything.

The ten turned their backs and whispered in a circle. Then one of them came up to Tullio and said, "Well, I guess you're right. It's your problem."

They left.

That night Edvige's window opened two inches, a hand appeared, and dropped a rose into the street. It was the first time the window had been opened after I don't know how many serenades. How could we be sure that the white hand that dropped the rose was really Edvige's and not one of the servants playing a cruel joke on Tullio? Edvige was the daughter of a very rich man, and they had lots of servants.

Tullio picked up the rose and kissed it like a lovesick fool.

On our way home I said to him, "In my opinion you're hamming it up worse than Amedeo Nazzari."

He smelled the rose and started to laugh. It was a strange laugh, a laugh that came from his stomach, gurgling, like a stream flowing over round stones, the laugh of a woman, and not a good woman at that. He looked at me like I was the jerk who didn't understand anything. It's true, I didn't understand. I had a funny feeling that something bad was going to happen.

Next day, on the table, we found a pitcher of milk and six eggs along with the usual bread, wine, and cheese. There was a piece of lard too.

The whole farse lasted twenty days — twenty nights of serenades, twenty mornings of sleeping late, twenty free meals. On the twentieth night Edvige's garden gate had been left open. Tullio went in. Cesarino and I played our songs in the street, as usual. An hour passed, two hours. Finally, he came out.

Sergio Atzeni

As soon as we got away from Edvige's window, Tullio pulled out a pair of woman's underwear, bloomers, you know, the kind that go all the way down to the knee. He waved them in the air, like a flag. Then he folded them up and tucked them into his jacket pocket, right over his heart.

"The hunt is finished," he said, "tomorrow we shall celebrate."

Next morning there was only bread and wine on the table. Tullio opened his trunk and got out his old party suits, all dusty and full of moth holes, though at one time they must have been considered very elegant attire indeed. The suit he gave me was too short and a little tight. But back in those days in Marmilla nobody worried about such particulars, and once we were all dressed we looked like three elegant gentlemen on their way to a wedding.

Arriving in the Piazza della Chiesa we spotted those field hands who'd stopped us one night in the street, now all cleaned up and decked out in their Sunday best, standing on the church steps. In the Piazza itself were about ten miners dressed in work clothes. I recognized one of them, that Ulysses character I told you about who invited us to the wedding at the beginning of the story.

I said, "Cesarino, let's get out of here." But no, Cesarino loved madness and madmen — they say it's a common trait among musicians — and no one was crazier than Tullio Saba. This was the grand finale, Cesarino wouldn't miss this one for his life. He was the leader of the band, so if he stayed, I stayed too.

The people came out of the church. A lot of them, a hundred, well-dressed — it was a wedding. The bride in her white wedding gown — it was Edvige, the beast. Many had noticed Tullio, and their glances shifted from him to the group of miners in the Piazza. The wedding party proceeded onward, paraded right in front of us, pretending to be oblivious to our presence. Then came the bride and groom. Tullio whipped out Edvige's bloomers and threw them in the groom's face. The bride fainted, and the groom let Tullio have it.

They massacred us.

That Ulysses had a stick and started swinging it like a maniac. He was on our side! He knocked ten of our adversaries to the ground. But there were just too many of them.

Tullio ended up with two eyes like eggplants. Cesarino had a bad cut on the nape of his neck that was bleeding all over the place. I received a compound fracture to my thigh bone. Three months I spent in the hospital, and I've had a limp ever since.

I quit the band, took an exam, and got my license as private music teacher. I don't regret a thing and I don't blame anybody. I knew that whole adventure was bound to turn out bad, but I didn't abandon my friends. I hope I've been a decent music teacher for the kids of Gonnos, that's all.

Thinking it over, that was the best year of my life. My children know that story by heart. You know how many times I've told it to them?

25

That Communist? They talked about him too much while he was alive, and now you want to dig him up? Forget it, get out of here!

I got nothing to say. I was director of personnel at the mine when I knew him. I can tell you this: that man was rotten to the core.

Sergio Atzeni

Edvige Zuddas? Yes, she's my wife. So what?
Edvige, there's a Commie journalist with an earring out here who's asking about Tullio Saba. You got news?
Hear that, she said, "No news."
You didn't hear?
You hear me?
Communists, Edie. I'll get rid of 'em.
Get out of here!
Journalists, bastards every one of 'em.
You ought to be thankful I got manners, otherwise I'd kick your ass right on out of here.
And take off that earring you queer!

26

I knew him, yeah. In those years he was a famous politician. He lived in one of my aunt Manuela's furnished rooms. A pig, like every other man I've ever known. As soon as I bent over to make his bed, he'd come up and grab me from behind, start rubbing himself against me.
He was always hard too.
I didn't want my aunt to get the wrong idea, so I never called for help.
And he took advantage of this.

27

He was quite a handsome man, not tall, but with very expressive eyes. I didn't know him personally. I often went to his speeches,

Bakunin's Son

though, and he explained complicated issues using simple words. At one speech I met Raffaele, whom I eventually married. He's been a good husband so far, I can't complain.

28

As a carabiniere I considered him my enemy, but as a man I respected him. He knew what he was doing, he did his job. Not like those rebels a few years ago, the only things they knew were guns and killing. Nor like certain others on TV today, who claim to be revolutionaries but in reality have one hand in the cookie jar like all the rest, and if there's a vacant post to be filled, their kids get first shot at it, then their kids' friends, relatives, and so on.

I don't recall that your man ever hurt anyone, or put his snout in the trough, if you know what I mean.

I followed him quite a bit back in the 50s. He really moved, all over the place. He pushed the farmers to occupy and farm untilled lands, to raise crops and reap a great harvest.

I don't know anything else about him, though. Apart from that period, I never much bothered with politics. I preferred petty crime, a whole 'nother thing.

What I really love, besides my wife and kids, is soccer. My wife keeps saying next time the national team scores I'll drop dead of a heart attack. One thing for sure, there hasn't been another striker like Gigi Riva.

But I can tell you one thing about Saba: he and the rest of the politicians of his time were a lot cleaner than today's politicians, believe me, that's the word of a carabiniere. And don't

Sergio Atzeni

listen to anybody who says the carabinieri are stupid. We ourselves are the ones who make up all the jokes about carabinieri, because we have a sense of irony. I used to know a carabiniere who could reason way better than many of the artists and thinking men of this country, the ones you see on TV.

29

Those were mixed up years. The perception of reality was much different than it is today.

I'll give you an example to illustrate my point: you know where the INA building is? The one before you get to Piazza Amendola, at the end of Via Roma, across from the little square where the harbor office is. In '46 they offered it to us for peanuts. We held a meeting of the Regional Secretariat to discuss the matter. Luisa Raccis said to buy. Now there was a woman with business in her blood. She knew how to make a deal. Years later she left the party and became a successful real estate agent — if I'm not mistaken, you bought your house from her, right? Instead, Velio Spano said, "Forget about it, after the revolution it'll all be ours, and not only the INA building, but all of Via Roma as well, without spending a lira."

Luisa Raccis wouldn't change her mind. Buy. She was skeptical. She knew there was no revolution at hand.

But I believed Velio. I was a boy from the provinces. My opposition to Fascism was kidstuff. I limited myself to maintaining contact with the few comrades I knew, distributing flyers at the Eden, throwing them from the balcony of the movie theater. That movie theater was subsequently torn down.

Yes, I had a little schooling — while I was in jail. But it wasn't much. They taught us the basics of Communist thought.

Bakunin's Son

Velio represented the big, unknown world. He'd lived firsthand all that was just a myth for us — the war in Spain, the struggle against the Nazis in Tunisia, twice condemned to death, wanted by the SS, followed Rommel's troops and communicated their movements to the English by radio. How could we not believe what he said? The revolution was near, right around the corner.

...In those years we faced a tough battle. Forty-nine saw our defeat both in the mines and at FIAT. We spread to the country, we organized movements to occupy the land. We shook half the island, from Marmilla to Sarrabus to Sassari.

It was then that I met Tullio Saba. As far as political leanings went, he was an anarchist. Sardinia has a long anarchic tradition, perhaps linked to the solitary existences led by the shepherds and bandits, or the stubborn individualism of the craftsmen.

Anyhow, Tullio became a Communist.

After 1950 we understood that what lay before us was not a single wall to tear down, but rather a long hard path to trod.

Tullio ran for a seat in the Second Regional Council, 1953. He won the hearts of everyone in Guspini and the surrounding villages and was elected by a landslide. As it turned out though, life as a parliamentarian didn't exactly appeal to him. When it came down to it, he really didn't agree with the direction in which the party was moving either. He preferred the hot years — he was a rousing speaker, but mainly a man of action. Also a bit of a ham if you want to know the truth. He rarely showed up when the council was in session, and when he did he'd dress up like a clown, with a blue zoot suit, yellow socks, red pointy shoes, stuff like that.

Then he got sick. In his final days he didn't want to see anyone. He died in silence.

Sergio Atzeni

My opinion? Well, I knew others like him, for whom the revolution was a romantic dream. But when it came to a question of patience and sitting down at the table and thinking the whole thing out calmly, he died on us. Only him, luckily.

We survivors worked to build an Italy better than there was in the past.

Not by ourselves? Be that as it may.

Worse than before? Wasn't our fault.

If Velio had been right would we have been worse off today? History's never been based on ifs.

Surely, by the questions you ask, you must have quit being a Communist.

Now why are you wearing that earring?

30

It's both a very beautiful and very painful memory. Beautiful because it's filled with such wonderful feelings, painful because of how it finished. I don't like to talk about it. And you, you're so young, why are you going around chasing after long-forgotten stories? Why aren't you thinking about girls instead. If I was your age I sure wouldn't be wasting my time digging up the dead. Are you a journalist? I've never seen you on TV. The guy on TV has a face like a boiled fish, what's his name?

You're strange. Hasn't anybody ever told you that before? No, it's not because of your earring — even Maradona has one.

If I tell you my story, it's not going to be printed in the *Unione*, is it? If it is, I won't tell you anything.

In all my life I've only told it to one person — my best friend.

Alright, you seem a little crazy to me, and I've always had a

Bakunin's Son

soft spot for nuts — it's normal people who scare me. I'll tell you.

I lived in Giba till I was 14. There were 17 of us, counting mother, father, brothers, and sisters, and two sisters' fiancés. My father only had one leg, he'd lost the other in the war. Sometimes he got drunk and beat us. The best part of my life at home was the picture novels, I'm not ashamed to admit it. I always had my nose in one of those picture novels — that's how I learned to read and write.

One day two men came in a car. Back then it was rare to see a car in Giba, since everybody still went to work by ox-drawn wagon. I ran into the street to see, together with all the rest of the kids of the village. I can't tell you how amazed and afraid I was when I saw those two men enter our house.

They were looking for a clean, hard-working girl to look after a sick man back in Cagliari. I spoke up immediately, without even thinking, and said, "I'll go." They looked at me, were a little doutful at first, then decided I'd be okay. Maybe they were in a hurry.

Then my father butted in and said he wanted thirty-thousand lire for me. If they hadn't taken me on account of my father and his thirty-thousand lire, I don't know what I would have done. I think I would have beaten him.

They paid without batting an eye, and we left.

They hardly said anything about what I was supposed to do. Just that I had to take care of a sick man, cook for him, clean the house, help him. I imagined a little old grandpa with white hair.

That's how I came to Cagliari the first time. I felt a great stir in my soul. The same that a girl living in Cagliari today might experience if she suddenly found herself in New York City, about to begin a new life. Everything seemed so incredibly

Sergio Atzeni

big, beautiful, fantastic, wonderful, chaotic, crazy, brightly-colored. People, voices, store windows, cars, horns blowing, street lights, a dream. Everybody walked so fast, and the sidewalks were jam-packed. We walked under the porticoes in Via Roma in the midst of a great throng. I started crying. The two men asked me if I wanted to go back home. I shook my head no, and to convince them I even tried to laugh, like a fool.

I was just a girl. That day was probably the most beautiful in my life. I wouldn't have to put up with daddy's whipping my backside anymore. I was about to experience the adventures of a big, bright city.

My gaze wandered from the people over to the huge ships in the harbor. Each ship with a different flag.

The house was in Su Brugu, two floors, with a very narrow staircase. It's still there today. On the ground floor was a tobacconist's shop. That's still there too.

As we walked up the stairs, they told me the man would be back that night. In the meantime I could do what I wanted. "Don't get lost if you go out," they warned me.

Well, I thought, the old man mustn't be too sick if he can go out. That was one more reason for me to be happy.

I explored the apartment with great curiosity. Two of the rooms had windows. There was a bedroom with a cot and a mattress that also functioned as a kitchen, with stove, sink, table and cupboard. This room opened to a great balcony where the bathroom and a pantry were located. The middle room had no windows and contained only two bookcases covered with dust. The front room had a window that looked out onto the street. In this room there was a bed, a closet, sink, and bedpan. There was also a wicker basket filled with oranges and tangerines.

Bakunin's Son

It was a poor house, but you should have seen the one I came from.

I tried to imagine what my master, the sick man, would be like.

I went to the window and looked down at the street, the people passing by, the cars' headlights. I stayed there a while, munching on oranges and tangerines. I spit the seeds out the window. Soon it got dark.

The street lights lit up. Gradually the crowds disappeared. There was hardly anyone left, except for an occassional individual or group of two or three going in or out of a door across the street. I figured it was a tavern, and I wasn't mistaken.

The evening was mild, a gentle breeze blew, the city had a sweet smell to it. Behind the top of a tall building, looking towards the port, I noticed a silver halo beginning to rise, and in a few minutes a splendid crescent moon was smiling in the sky.

A man appeared down on the sidewalk. He took slow, precise steps, his head held high. He had on a strange overcoat that fluttered in the breeze. He was young, and as he approached I was able to distinguish the features of his face, a strikingly handsome face. He didn't see me, just looked straight ahead. Maybe he was thinking. He came in our door. I heard his footsteps on the stairs. The key turned in the lock. It was my master.

The first words he spoke to me were, "Have you eaten?"

"Oranges," I answered.

He smiled. What a smile. Beautiful. Good. White teeth, little and straight.

In his arms he held a package. He opened it. Inside was a taccula, a piece of roast goat and a bottle of red wine. It was the tastiest dinner of my life.

Sergio Atzeni

I laughed and laughed. Then I inquired, "They told me you were sick. That can hardly be true."

By the scowl he gave me I knew I wasn't supposed to bring up that subject again.

He seemed like a boy to me. His hair was black and tangled. The color of his bright eyes changed with the seasons — on certain summer days they were as yellow as honey, during the winter they were brown as chestnuts. He liked my baked artichokes, and chick-pea soup with rosemary, stuffed chicken.... Why are you making me tell this story? I don't want to.

I was with him for sixteen months. During the last twelve he never left the house. He would just sit in the room with no windows, reading or pretending to read. He spoke very little. Once in a while he smiled.

I would have done anything he'd asked. But he didn't ask. I was a virgin and I stayed that way. Not even a kiss, he was nothing less than chaste. I loved him from the moment I saw him walking down the street, with his overcoat blowing in the breeze.

I think he loved me too, like a sister.

The pain kept him awake day and night. I stayed by him, to keep him company, or to get him some fruit or a drink of water if he wanted, and I wiped his forehead when he was hot. I didn't sleep very much myself, but when I did I dreamed about him. I longed to share his pain and ease his suffering. I asked myself the usual, unanswerable questions that one asks when the injustice of sickness and death is consuming the person they love. I prayed to that god I remember only in times of agony, I implored him to put an end to the torture that had devastated the face of the man I so loved, the face that made him unrecognizable and frightening.

Bakunin's Son

One morning, at the first light of dawn, he recalled a childhood memory — that of having listened to his father's confused interpretations of Darwin and evolution and thinking how he would study and become a natural scientist. The city was silent, a ray of gray light shone on his ironic smile and he laughed to himself like a baby.

One of his last nights, he said, "I have one regret...I don't even know if it's right.... One time, my best friend, who was more than a brother to me, asked me for a gun.... I didn't have one...but I knew a smuggler who did....

"I knew my friend didn't want that gun to keep dogs away.... I gave him the address...he bought a gun.... No, I wouldn't do it again. Would I do it again?"

Another night he said, "I wanted sharp colors, violent emotions, impossible challenges...."

I asked him one morning, "Are you ready to meet God?"

His eyes were slits, he managed a sneer with his big lips, a half smile, almost sinister, and replied, "I've never met God before."

"Haven't you ever prayed for yourself, for others?"

"My mother used to pray, and my father used to always go around repeating the words of a Russian anarchist, 'Work is our prayer....'"

I prayed for him though.

His face was contorted, like the branch of an olive tree. Then he stopped breathing and lay flat. It looked as if he were smiling.

The window was open. Sunlight flooded the room, the worn sheets shined like mother-of-pearl, the breeze carried with it the

Sergio Atzeni

smells of the market — fresh-caught fish, oranges, vanilla, plucked chickens.

He left me the house in his will.

I gave it to his friends.

For a year afterwards I felt a sharp, excruciating pain in my stomach, right where he had felt his pain. Then it passed. I haven't had a bad life.

31

In the mid-fifties after a nine month draught that had reduced the fields to dusty deserts, there was a flood in Sarrabus. That's how nature is with this land. Ferocious, without measure, from one extreme to the other, as if it wanted to continually test the patience of the inhabitants. Ten days of pouring rain and hail in September. All the streams were overflowing, water rushed through the village streets, dissolving the mud walls of the houses. Then came the wind. Fruit trees and oaks crashed violently upon the roofs. Many people died, mostly old folks and children. There was a great commotion and a great solidarity arose. All Italy began sending supplies to help the flood victims. A system for distributing the goods had to be organized. Tullio Saba was nominated to head the project. As the first shipments arrived he requisitioned a warehouse down at the port, and started to stockpile the stuff that wasn't immediately necessary — moth-eaten shirts, itchy wool sweaters, typewriters without keys or ribbons, worn out fur collars, heavy wool overcoats stinking of moth balls, empty glass jars without lids, new Ziess lenses for half glasses, roasting pans encrusted black, alarm clocks that would have cost more to repair than to buy new, a railway car full of rusty old

Bakunin's Son

mufflers, ten cases of brand new fezes, and so much other junk donated by so many charitable souls. They'd cleaned out their attics and garages for us. As soon as the first warehouse was filled, Tullio requisitioned another.

The emergency ended and the owners began pushing to have their warehouses back. Tullio didn't know what to do with all that accumulated stuff and began to lose hope. He considered throwing the whole lot of it into the sea, in the harbor, but he didn't have the money to pay the longshoremen to dump it. Finally a buyer showed up, a Neapolitan, exactly one year after the flood. He only wanted the wool and the scrap iron but pitied Tullio and took everything for the price he had offered for the wool alone. In three nights a troop of his workers loaded the whole, lock stock and barrel, onto a cargo ship — I remember its name: "Tonight Tiziana at Mergellina." The Neapolitan left and Tullio found himself with a nice wad of dough in his pocket. For a couple of days he grappled with two distinct possibilities. Either go to Sarrabus and make a gift of one hundred lire to each of the twenty or thirty families, and one hundred lire was nothing to sneeze at in those days, or keep everything for himself.

In the meantime another problem — he had gotten a lady comrade pregnant. Now he had no intention of marrying her, but he didn't want to send her to one of those women who perform abortions on the kitchen table.

So he decided to take the money and ship off. I think he went to Peru. At least that's what people say. He never came back here, that's for sure.

They told you he died in Cagliari? In a house in Su Brugu? Bullshit!

Sergio Atzeni

Who told you? A woman? Women…instead of simply accepting the fact that Tullio Saba did a really rotten thing, they prefer making up some story and imagine he's dead…. He had a way with women alright. They swarmed around him like flies on shit. I don't know what it was, though I myself've never understood women — it's no coincidence that at my age I'm still single! They say it's because I'm greedy. Bullshit! It's just that the woman who could make a cuckold out of me hasn't been born yet.

The lady comrade Tullio Saba abandoned? The kid? Well, she married a real good man and the kid grew up healthy and strong. He was the spitting image of his father, same body, same face, but mostly his eyes and character.

It's you.

Why are you so pale?

Nobody ever told you before?

32

Well, that's what's left of Tullio Saba in the memories of those who knew him. Everything they said I recorded on my AIWA portable; everything on tape I transcribed without adding or omitting anything. I don't know what the truth is, if there is a truth. Maybe some of those interviewed lied on purpose. Or maybe they all really believe what they said. Or maybe they just invented a few particulars, here and there, to spice up their stories. The most likely hypothesis is that the facts have been distorted, transformed, given a fable-like quality by the veil of time that changes the people as well as their recollections.

*This Book Was Completed on July 25, 1996 at
Italica Press, New York, New York & Was
Set in Galliard. This Printing is on
60-lb White Opaque Vellum
Paper by BookMobile,
St. Paul, MN,
U. S. A.*
✶ ✶
✶